More Daddy

A Daddies Inc Novel

Lucky Moon

Contents

Keep in Touch

Thanks for stopping by!

If you want to keep in touch and receive a **FREE BOX SET** as a thank you for signing up, just head to the link here: http://eepurl.com/gYVLJ1

I'll shower with you love and affection, giving you **insider information** on my series, plus all kinds of other **treats**. My newsletter goes out once a week and contains giveaways, polls, exclusive content, and lots more fun besides.

Also, you can get in touch with me at luckymoonromance@gmail.com or find me on Facebook. I love hearing from fans!

Lucky x o x

Chapter One

KIERA

FAIRYTALES WERE SUCH BALONEY.

Poor girl meets wealthy man who whisks her off for a life of happily ever after?

Beautiful princess meets ugly beast who turns out to be the most handsome hunk in the universe?

Sleepyhead finally awakens from her long sleep by a guy who just happens to be the man of her dreams?

Yeah, right.

Kiera Stark knew that life just didn't work out like that. Poor girls stayed poor. Beautiful princesses married handsome princes — until the princes traded them in for a younger model. The man of your dreams? Well, he just didn't exist.

And yet, here she was, at her best friend Daisy's wedding, in a lemon-colored bridesmaids gown, with white flowers woven into her hair, like she was some kind of... romantic. She hadn't believed Daisy at first when she'd announced that she was getting married in a castle. Like, a real proper castle in the countryside of *Scotland*.

But of *course* she was. Daisy was marrying her handsome billionaire, Montague, and a fairytale wedding was practically expected of them.

Kiera didn't want to rain on her best friend's parade, so she had dressed up like a lemon meringue pie, walked behind Daisy down the aisle, and laughed politely at the funny bits in the best man's speech. She had eaten her fancy dinner, including all the green bits, and she had danced to the strange Scottish music.

And now she was bouncing up and down in the big inflatable bounce house which Daisy had ordered to go in the grand entrance hall of the big red sandstone castle. A bouncy castle inside a real one. That had to be a metaphor for something.

As Kiera bounced around with Daisy, she found herself feeling worried about her best friend. Sooner or later, Montague was probably going to leave Daisy. Sure, he seemed like a good guy right now, but people changed. They always changed. They changed, and they let each other down.

Kiera's other best friend, Peach, waved excitedly at them from the sidelines. Peach's relationship with billionaire Isaac had started out as fake, but now it was real. Her case was even more tragic. She wasn't just married — she had a *baby* on the way. A baby! Peach was convinced she'd found everlasting happiness.

But Kiera knew better.

Isaac was going to leave Peach, just like Montague was going to leave Daisy. Because that's how real life worked. People messed up big time. People abandoned each other. People got screwed over.

Poor, poor Peach. Stuck at home holding the baby.

Kiera bounced higher and higher, trying to rise above her worries.

I wish I could just stay in here forever.

Bounce, bounce, bounce.

Nothing bad can ever happen to you in a bounce house.

"What on earth... are you... thinking about, Kiera?" Daisy panted as she jumped around in her wedding dress like an acrobat. "Your face is all screwy-uppy. Wait. Did you have two glasses of champagne tonight? You always get maudlin after a second drink."

Kiera shook her head, but in truth, Daisy was right. Her friend knew her so well! She *had* had two drinks. And now she *did* feel maudlin. She should have stuck to the milkshakes like Peach.

"I'm, er, just concentrating on bouncing," Kiera lied. "Seeing how high I can go."

"Oooh, sounds like you just challenged me to a competition!" said Daisy, laughing. "You be the judge, Peach!"

Peach grinned, obviously happy to be included. Being pregnant made it harder to join in with their fun. "Okay. Good luck, contestants!"

As the two girls started bouncing as high as they possibly could, Kiera began to loosen up. She had been having trouble getting into Little Space since her friends had both found their Daddies. They were often busy, and it was hard to play games and lean into her Little side — or, more precisely, her Middle side — when she was alone. But being here with her friends, jumping, felt good. It felt safe.

Up! Down! Up! Down!

Kiera felt the years peeling away from her like layers of old paint, revealing the bare core of her soul beneath.

"Wheee!" she cried out.

"Am I winning?" panted Daisy. "Peach? Am I... winning?" Daisy's cheeks had gone an adorable shade of pink. She was hot and sweaty in that big dress, but she looked happier than ever before. Her wedding gown was an exact replica of Cinderella's from the original movie. That was Daisy all over: a Disney princess.

Maybe... things would be okay for her?

"Hey, Daze," Kiera panted, almost as out of breath as her friend now. "I'm happy for you, you know?" She genuinely meant it. It always felt easier to see the good in things when she started to slip into Little Space. "You and Montague make the best couple."

"Hey!" Peach called from the sidelines, waving around a strawberry-colored lollipop that she had just picked up from a passing silver tray. "What about me and Isaac?"

Kiera laughed. "Sorry, Peachy Pop! You and Daddy Isaac make the best couple too."

It felt good to be positive. Even if that miserable voice was still trying to make itself heard deep inside of her.

Peach smiled, happily sucking on her lollipop as Isaac walked up behind her and put his arms around her growing belly. She was five months pregnant now and she was definitely showing. She'd grown rounder all over, but Isaac didn't seem to mind. In fact, he seemed to like it. He was always offering Peach some snack or other. Normally something healthy, but he let her have treats too. He was quite an indulgent Daddy. He whispered something in her ear and Kiera was sure she caught the word *ass*.

Kiera watched Isaac's hands stroking Peach's tummy. She couldn't imagine having something growing inside her. It was hard enough being responsible for her own life, let alone someone else's too.

"Hmmm, Kiera looks distracted again," said Daisy.

"Looks like you're the winner, Daisy!" called out Peach.

Daisy pumped her arms in the air victoriously. "Yes! I rule!"

Kiera slumped down on the rubbery floor of the bounce house, pretending to be a sore loser. "I guess it *is* your wedding day," she joked. "So I thought I'd better let you win."

Just then, there was the sound of bagpipes.

"Eek, it's time to cut the cake!" squealed Daisy.

She practically leaped off the bounce house and skipped over to Montague, who was deep in conversation with his best man, Bastion.

Bastion was probably being rude about something or someone. He normally was. To call the man a rogue was an understatement. He drank too much, he went to strip bars, and he even *apparently* jerked off in his office. Gross.

Still, all of that aside... Kiera couldn't deny how hot he looked in that kilt.

Who knew Bastion had Scottish ancestry? His family name — Barclay — even had its own tartan. Yellow with black stripes. That was about right. Yellow and black, like a stinging, poisonous, insect. Bastion Barclay was a danger to everyone, including himself.

Yeah, she was much safer in here, inside these lovely squishy walls. The world out there was a dangerous place.

Kiera started to bounce all on her own, as everyone else waited for the cake. It was so busy out there. Half the people from the Daddies Inc. offices were here, all flown over on Montague's private jet. A bit overwhelming being around so many people. Kiera normally preferred to be on her own.

Just then, the bagpipes stopped as the cake was wheeled out on a trolley. It was *huge*. There must have been at least twelve tiers. It was covered in white icing with pink rosebuds all over it.

But Kiera's eyes kept wandering over to something else. Someone else.

Bastion.

In that kilt.

Why were kilts so freaking sexy? They shouldn't be. But they were. Oh boy, they were.

She eyed Bastion's thick, muscular thighs peeping out from below that... masculine skirt.

She wondered if it was true what people said: that *true* Scotsmen didn't wear anything under their kilts. Was Bastion a true Scotsman?

Trying not to stare at Bastion's crotch, she moved her gaze upward and took in the rest of him. His athletic build looked good in that crisp white shirt and suit jacket. His short, graying hair and silvery beard looked perfectly distinguished. He definitely looked like more of a Daddy than either Montague or Isaac... and yet he acted nothing like one.

Bastion was the most obnoxious, dick-obsessed, alcohol-swilling meanie Kiera had ever met. Every time he and Kiera ended up close to one another, Bastion had something shitty to say to her. A nasty comment here. A strong opinion there. It was like he did it on purpose, just to get to her.

But right now, he was on the other side of the room. She was in her safe little bounce house. So, it was okay to look at him. Looking wasn't dangerous. Looking couldn't hurt her—

"Ow!"

Kiera had been so distracted that she had jumped right onto the wall of the bounce house, and fell down, bumping her head.

"Shoot," she whispered.

Luckily, she hadn't shouted loud enough to draw any attention to herself.

Her head was throbbing, though. Rubbing her temple, she got off the inflatable structure and went to look for a quiet corner to wallow in.

"Never should have had those drinks," she said to herself quietly.

Just then, she felt a tap on her shoulder. She whipped around, and saw the cause of her sore head standing there glaring at her. Maybe not glaring. Maybe... staring? Frowning in concern?

"Kiera," said Bastion, his voice so deep it seemed to make her bones vibrate. "You really shouldn't drink alcohol on the bouncy castle."

"I wasn't," said Kiera, pouting. "I drank *before* I got on the bouncy castle."

Bastion gave her a look. The sort of look that told her she was being pedantic.

"I only had a couple drinks anyway," she mumbled. "I'm not drunk." She looked at Bastion's shirt, which was a little disheveled close-up. She noticed a pinkness around the rim of his eyes. The scent of whiskey on his breath. "*You're* the one who's drunk, Bastion."

Bastion looked down at her. "I only had a couple drinks too," he replied moodily. He made air quotes with his fingers when he said the word "couple." Cheeky as ever.

Kiera rubbed her head again. "Why did you come over here, Bastion? To mock me?"

Bastion shook his head. "Nope. I came to help you find an ice pack."

Kiera waited for the nasty little comment to follow, but there wasn't one. Hmm. Maybe Bastion really did want to help her. There was a first time for everything.

"Come on," he told her. "This way."

Before she knew what was happening, he'd grabbed her by the hand and was leading her out of the main hall in search of an ice pack.

"I don't know if ancient castles have ice packs just lying around in them..." she said. "And honestly, my head really isn't that sore."

Bastion dragged her down a long corridor full of old oil paintings and empty coats of armor. There were all sorts of weapons hanging on the walls, too. Spears and daggers and old-looking rifles. It would be scary to get lost in a place like this on her own. Somehow, she felt safe with Bastion. Even though everything about the guy screamed *danger*.

"Here," said Bastion, pulling her into an empty room. "This should work."

They were in the staff kitchen, but there was nobody in there. The staff must have all been out in the main hall, walking around with lollipops on silver platters or helping with the cake. Bastion didn't seem to care that this was their domain. He strode through the kitchen like he owned the place, quickly locating a freezer and pulling out a bag of ice. He wrapped it in a dishcloth and took it over to Kiera.

"Keep it there for five minutes," he told her. "Let's go find someplace to sit down."

Kiera held Bastion's homemade ice pack to her head. "This is freezing. Can I just do one minute?"

Bastion didn't answer. He was dragging her again, this time into an empty drawing room with plush recliner couches and a roaring fire.

"Holy mackerel," said Kiera with a whistle. "This place is *fancy*."

The ceiling was vaulted, with gold details. The walls had frescoes all over them. Flowers and cherubs and windswept shores. A large stone fireplace with lions sculpted into it was at the far end, and Bastion made Kiera sit on a red velvet couch in front of it. For the briefest moment, *she* felt like the princess.

"You feeling alright?" he asked, sitting beside her. "No dizziness? No confusion?"

I'm confused about why you're being nice to me. Does that count?

"How many fingers am I holding up?" Bastion asked, showing her two digits.

"Four-hundred and ninety-eight," she said, going cross-eyed on purpose.

"Don't test me."

"Two," she told him, rolling her eyes. "Seriously. I don't need this thing." She pulled the ice pack away from her head, but Bastion's large hand grabbed hers, pushing the ice pack against her temple. He left his hand there, letting her feel how strong he was.

She stopped struggling against him, and started to enjoy the sensation of his heavy palm pressing down on her. If only Bastion were as kind as he was hot...

Slightly embarrassed, Kiera started to look around the room, trying to find a topic of conversation. Should she talk about the chandelier? The large Persian rug? The painting of the cherub on the wall, its bare ass gleaming in the evening light?

"You look uncomfortable," said Bastion. "Are you in pain, or is it because of me?" Bastion moved his hand away from hers.

Instantly, Kiera felt like she wanted Bastion's hand to go back. "I'm just surprised you're being nice to me right now," she said. "Didn't have you down as a knight in shining armor."

"You don't have *anyone* down as a knight in shining armor," Bastion told her. Then, before she had the chance to question that, he added: "Anyway, I saw you bump your head and wanted to help. That's all."

A thought occurred to Kiera. She had bumped her head because she'd been staring at Bastion. Had he been staring at her too?

Nah.

That'd be ridiculous. He was a successful billionaire who looked dangerously hot in a kilt. She was... well, she was a blue-haired punk with a failing bubble bath business. Even calling it a "business" was optimistic. It was more like a hobby. A pipe dream.

"Is my time up?" she asked impatiently. "I think I'm getting brain freeze."

"Three more minutes," said Bastion firmly. Then, softening, he added: "How about we play a game?"

"You and me, play a game?" scoffed Kiera. "You must be drunk."

Bastion blinked but didn't say anything. "Never have I ever," he told her. "You start."

"Okay, this is *definitely* a game drunk people play," said Kiera. "But fine. Never have I ever... stolen anything."

"Good," said Bastion, quick as a whip. "Never have I ever cheated on someone."

"Wait, you haven't?" said Kiera. "That surprises me."

"Your go," said Bastion insistently.

"Never have I ever had a million pounds in my bank account." She flung an accusing look at Bastion.

"Never have I ever gone more than two days without taking a shower," Bastion teased back.

Kiera scowled. "I'm actually really clean."

Bastion looked at her. "Oh yeah? What's the longest you've gone without taking a shower, then?"

Kiera swallowed. "I'm not saying."

"I knew it!"

"Stop being cruel," Kiera said. Then, without missing a beat, she said accusingly: "Never have I ever gone to a strip club."

"Never have I ever gotten a tattoo," Bastion said, giving that same look back to her.

"Never have I ever masturbated at work."

Bastion looked shocked, then, in a low voice, he said: "Never have I ever spanked someone's ass in a castle."

The silence hung thickly between them.

"Are you saying you want to spank my ass, Bastion?" she asked in a whisper.

Bastion's eyes lingered on her. "I've thought about it."

"You think I'm a bad girl?"

"I think you're a *very* bad girl."

Kiera bit her lip. "Well, I think you're a *very* nasty man."

Why was this turning her on? Bastion was her nemesis. He was the grumpiest grump, the meanest meanie. And he was the hottest man in a kilt she'd ever seen...

She threw down her ice pack. "I should go."

"You still have another minute left," Bastion warned her. "Put the ice pack back on, young lady."

Kiera shook her head adamantly, then stood up. "Nah. I don't wanna."

"Put it on, and go and stand in the naughty corner," he told her. His voice was unwavering. Commanding.

Kiera had a rebellious streak. She had always assumed she would make a terrible submissive because she hated playing by the rules. But the moment she heard Bastion speak to her like that, she felt like putty in his hands. She found herself picking up the ice pack, holding it to her head, and going to stand in the one corner of the room that wasn't occupied by a statue or a stuffed animal.

"I take it this is the naughty corner?" she asked, looking back. She was expecting to see Bastion sitting on the couch she'd just gotten up from, but she squeaked when she saw him right behind her.

"Your safeword is 'thistle,'" he said into her ear.

She looked straight ahead of her, still holding the ice pack to her temple. She noticed that the wall had small purple thistles painted on it.

"Your head hurts for even a minute and you use that safeword," he told her. "And if you want me to stop for any other reason, you use it too. Understood?"

Kiera nodded. "My head feels fine now. I could probably put the ice pack dow—"

"Sssh," urged Bastion, lifting the back of her dress. "No talking unless it's the safeword."

Kiera swallowed as she felt Bastion's thick fingers sliding into the hem of her panties and pulling them down. Strictly speaking, she wasn't wearing proper panties. Kiera didn't do girly unless she had to. Underneath this lemon meringue dress, she was wearing old gray boxers. Bit embarrassing, but Bastion didn't seem to care. Besides, he was pulling them down right now, revealing her bare bottom.

The ice on her head and the warmth of the fire on her bottom were an interesting mix. She couldn't deny it — this was fun. But Bastion wasn't really going to slap her ass, was he? What if someone walked in?

"Get ready," he said in a strange new voice. One she hadn't heard him use before. It was deep but there was a croak in it, like it was catching in his throat. Was he nervous? Excited? Angry?

Slap!

Out of nowhere, the pain spread across her buttock, red hot and tingling. It was such a shock that her arm fell to her side, no longer holding the ice up to her head, but surely a minute had gone by anyway...

She clenched her eyes tight shut, waiting for the next spank, but it didn't come.

"Why have you stopped, Bastion?" she taunted. "Is that all you can muster?"

Bastion's warm body pushed up against her back. She felt his heavy breath on her neck as he whispered: "I don't want to fight you, baby-girl... I want to fuck you."

Kiera's pulse quickened. This was very naughty. She knew it wasn't meant to happen like this. Daddies and Littles — or Middles — didn't meet via one-night stands. They had strict rules and protocols in place before anything like this happened. They had mutual respect and understanding. They had...

Holy *shit*, Bastion's hand was traveling up her thigh, sliding under her butt cheeks and seeking out her pussy from behind. She felt his fingertips brush her pussy lips, which were already wet with lust. How did it happen? How had this man turned her on so fast?

Then, his fingers stopped, as if waiting.

"Go on," Kiera urged him. "I dare you."

In less than a second, she felt Bastion's finger on her clit. Softly at first, circling her, getting to know the way she twitched. Then, his finger grew more sure of itself. It applied more pressure. Made quicker movements.

Kiera started to tremble uncontrollably with desire. She couldn't bear to overthink this, to stop and wonder what was going on, what she was going to do after the deed was done. All she cared about was feeling Bastion's hot, hard erection deep within her pussy.

But his erection hadn't made its way out of his pants yet. And if it didn't slide inside of her soon, she was going to come without it.

"I'm gonna..." Kiera gasped, her teeth chattering. "I'm gonna c... c..."

"Oh no you don't," said, pushing something oddly freezing against her clit.

What the...?

Of course. The *ice*.

It sent crackles of frosty cold darting around her pussy. Her brain didn't know what to make of it. The warmth of his fingers. The chill of the ice. The combination was making it hard to think, turning her into a bundle of sensations.

"Interesting fact about ice," Bastion growled behind her. "It prolongs your ability to withhold an orgasm. Meaning you stay turned on for longer."

Kiera bit down on her lip, riding the ice-cold waves of constant ecstasy.

I'm gonna have to come sooner or later.

No one can be this aroused forever.

Bastion pushed his body up against hers, pressing her into the naughty corner. She could feel his hard cock pressing into her. Or maybe that was his sporran? Who knew? Who cared?

She was... she was... she was... so... close...

"I'm gonna take the ice away in a moment, babygirl," said Bastion, still strumming her and freezing her all at once. "And when I do, I want you to come on Daddy's hand like a good girl."

Were they roleplaying?

Did he really see himself as her Daddy?

Again, who cared?

She was... she was.. she was... so... close...

Suddenly, Bastion took away the ice, and she was left with nothing but the warmth of his finger and the fire. The heat rushed to her pussy like it had been lit with touch paper. And then...

Explosion.

Explosion.

Explosion.

She came over and over again — or at least, it felt that way, because every time she thought she'd spasmed and shuddered enough, she spasmed and shuddered one last time. It was the deepest, richest, most wonderful orgasm of her whole life.

All the while, Bastion kept his fingers where they were, making sure that she rode every last wave of pleasure.

When she was done, his lips grazed the soft skin of her neck, and then he kissed her ear.

She shivered all the way down that side of her body.

"Well," she said, drunk with pleasure. "Are you gonna fuck me now?"

But Bastion didn't reply. In fact, she couldn't feel him anymore.

And when she turned around, she couldn't see him either.

Chapter Two

BASTION

H E HAD WANTED TO be the knight in shining armor. He had wanted to be the handsome prince.

But as he paced his plush room in the turret of the castle, he knew he had fucked up. The morning sun shone in through his window, doing everything it could to cheer him up, but it wasn't working. He'd felt terrible last night, and this morning, he felt even worse.

He shouldn't have done that with Kiera. It hadn't been his intention when he'd gone over to help her. He'd genuinely been concerned about her head. But the moment he started speaking to her, he could see that she was fine. It had only been a small bump on a soft bounce house.

But his protective streak had kicked in. He'd felt compelled to get that ice for her. Just to be on the safe side.

Being around her after a couple drinks had been dangerous, though.

He'd been into that girl since Day fucking One. The first time he saw her, with those defiant brown eyes and those wildly cute cheek dimples, he'd just known. That fuck-you attitude only made it worse. Her permanent scowl, that piercing protruding from her pouting lower lip, and that icy blue streak in her hair. So much sweetness and rebellion all rolled into one delicious, unique, beguiling package.

Obviously, she was way too young for him. And way too lovely.

Bastion was like an old, beat-up car. Barely even good enough to get you from A to B. Spilling engine oil wherever he went. Spluttering and stalling and rusty as hell.

When he'd sat with her last night, though, he'd been unable to contain himself. He'd felt years younger all of a sudden. He'd felt like anything was possible.

But he'd done it all wrong. Okay, he gave her a safeword, but everything was done out of order. They didn't have a contract, and he didn't know about her hard and soft limits. He didn't even know if she was into him. Most importantly of all, he wasn't her Daddy and he never would be.

Truth is, he'd never be anyone's Daddy.

Bastion walked over to the window and opened it for some air. He tried not to think about the phrase "erectile dysfunction." It was hard, ironically.

Truth was, Bastion was impotent.

Ever since his wife had left him, he couldn't get an erection. No actually, it was even longer ago than that. He couldn't get it for a year before she left him.

Of course, he'd had it all checked out by a doctor. A very good doctor, at that. But all that Doctor Ryker had diagnosed him with was stress. Offered to send him to a psychiatrist friend of his, but Bastion had refused. Didn't have time for that stuff. His cock was the problem, not his damn head. It was embarrassing enough having a limp dick, let alone seeing a shrink about it. He hadn't even talked about the issue with Montague or Isaac. He made this big show about jerking off in the office, but it was all a lie. He hadn't successfully jerked off in nearly two years. And definitely not in the office.

As for all the strip clubs he'd been going to since his wife had left him... those trips were just experiments. Desperate attempts to get hard. Desperate failures.

Last night, for the first time in forever, he felt a... spark down there.

A spark that he wanted *so fucking badly* to ignite.

Kiera was practically begging him for it.

But she wasn't thinking straight. She'd been drinking, even if she wasn't drunk. She was at a wedding. Emotions were running high. Plus, she hated him.

There was a reason for that, obviously. Plenty of reasons. He always said the wrong thing around her because she made him nervous. Something about that girl drove him crazy like no-one else. But he always ended up saying something that upset her, putting his foot in it. Probably the drink didn't help. Nor did his argumentative nature.

He took in a deep breath of Scottish air, trying to soothe his hangover.

He was queasy as hell, but the cool breeze felt good on his face.

Ah, Scotland.

There was nothing quite like the Scottish highlands. Bastion's father's family had come from this land originally, and although this was his first time here, it felt like a homecoming of sorts. The bleak beauty of Rannoch Moor, with its peat bogs and heather-clad hills. Gnarled pines, granite tors, shimmering lochs. A land of legend and drama. Of stags and whiskey.

Oh no. Better not to think about the whiskey.

Bastion took a long, deep breath.

There was so much more to life than drink. For so many years, life had passed him by in a blur. So many opportunities had been wasted. So many experiences had been screwed up.

He took his phone out of his pocket and pointed it at the wild view in front of him, then he took a snap. A reminder. A promise. From this day forward, he was giving it all up. It just wasn't worth it. If he ever wavered, he'd look back at this photograph and remember this feeling. Guilt. Shame. And hope.

His stomach gurgled. The breakfast banquet would be served in half an hour.

A good Scottish breakfast would settle his stomach. Eggs, bacon, sausages, toast, maybe even some black pudding or haggis. He couldn't handle the thought of seeing Kiera at the table without talking to her first, though. There was so much he needed to tell her.

That he was sorry for letting things happen.

That he was sorry for the disappearing act.

That he was stupidly attracted to her.

That he could never, ever be with her.

That she deserved someone who could actually put his dick inside her.

He had no idea how he'd find the words for all that stuff, but he had to try. So, dressed in blue jeans and a plaid shirt, looking much less dashing this morning than he had done at the wedding, he navigated the narrow corridors of the castle toward her room.

He knew where she was staying because Daisy had allocated everyone's rooms according to their spirit animals. She had stuck pictures of the animals on the doors. Bastion was staying in the honey badger room. Daisy said that he was a honey badger because he was a fierce competitor and never backed down in a fight. Apparently, Kiera was a camel. The heart of a traveler. Dignified and with great endurance. He knew that because he heard Kiera noisily complaining about it when they arrived. She said she wanted to be something cute or fierce, but Bastion knew that Kiera was a camel deep down. Adventurous and strong. Maybe she just hadn't realized it yet.

Finally, he found her door and tried not to laugh when he saw the photograph of a camel with its drooling tongue lolling out. He could see why Kiera might not have been delighted with that!

He composed himself and then knocked. As he waited for her to answer, terrible images flashed through his mind.

She had passed out on the floor with a concussion.

She had never made it back to her room last night and had wandered off onto the moors in the darkness.

She was in bed with someone else, his rock-hard cock deep in her open mouth, her sexy little piercing rubbing against his balls—

"Kiera."

Kiera looked surprised to see him. She was wearing purple sweatpants and a matching hoodie. She had neon green headphones on and slightly pink cheeks.

"Is this a bad time?" Bastion asked awkwardly.

"Nope," said Kiera. "I just got in from a run."

She opened the door a little wider, inviting him in, but the atmosphere between them wasn't comfortable. The icy climax he'd given her last night stood between them like a portcullis.

"A run?" said Bastion as he entered the room and closed the door behind him. "I thought you might be hungover."

"After two drinks?" Kiera said, breaking a smile. "Hardly."

"Pah. Young people," said Bastion, waving his hand dismissively.

"Did you... come here for any reason?" Kiera asked, her energy spiky and defensive. "I need to take a shower before breakfast. I like to shower frequently, in spite of what you might think."

Ouch.

"I came to apologize," he said, cutting to the chase. "I can assure you that nothing like that will ever happen again."

Kiera bit her lip. She paused a moment, and then said, "Good."

Bastion walked over to the window and instinctively opened it. He took a deep breath. "It's obvious to me," he said, "that you and I have some longstanding... feud. The fact that you don't like me is written all over your face, and... well, honestly, I'm not looking for commitment right now."

I'm putting up barriers to protect us both.

I could never satisfy you.

I'm afraid you'd abandon me.

Kiera shrugged. "Same."

Bastion nodded. "Okay. Well. That's... good."

Kiera blinked at him. It must have been cold out there this morning. Her dark eyes were watery from the breeze. Watery, and big, and thickly lashed.

God, she looked beautiful this morning.

He'd love to just end all this bullshit, drag her over to the castle window, bend her over, and squeeze his hot, hard dick between her thighs...

Except that he couldn't do it, even if he wanted to.

And for that reason, as well as so many others, he had to help the poor girl stay free.

"Is there anything else?" Kiera asked, putting her hands on her hips. "I have stuff to do."

Bastion swallowed. "No," he said. "That's it. I just wanted to check you were okay. That you slept alright, and feel fine after what happened."

And if you wanted me to, I'd provide you with the aftercare I should have provided you with last night.

"Bastion?" said Kiera, smiling sweetly.

"Yes?" His heart raced.

"You can go now."

Chapter Three

KIERA

BACK TO LIFE. BACK to reality. Back to a failing bubble bath business and a whole heap of existential doom.

Scotland had been like entering a portal into another world. Like going to the back of her closet and finding a magical snowy landscape of ice queens and mystical beings. It was a world where she and Bastion touched intimately, where haters became lovers... and then haters again.

Kiera frowned.

She hadn't told her friends what had happened in Scotland. Daisy was on her honeymoon vacation with Montague, anyway. He was taking her on a tour of the world's best theme parks.

Peach was here, at her apartment, but she was too busy being pregnant and in love to hear about Kiera's weird one-night stand. It felt so wrong and shameful to admit to it to someone who was so happy.

Not that what happened in Scotland *had* been a one-night stand exactly. You have to have actual penetration for that, don't you? More like a one-night... hand. It had only been his finger and some ice on her clit... Oh man, the way it had felt...

Ugh. The whole thing was Bastion's fault, obviously.

Kiera had been perfectly content being alone before he'd crashed into her life. A mixture of fire and ice. Hot and cold, just like him.

When he'd turned up outside her room the next morning, she'd been grateful for the apology, but honestly, the only thing he'd needed to apologize for was running off. Before that, what had happened between them had felt so special. He'd even called her Daddy. It had felt at that moment like he'd truly meant it...

Obviously not. He'd made things pretty clear.

I'm not looking for commitment right now.

She'd half-hoped that he was going to rip off her clothes and make her his that morning. But she'd been wearing her sweaty workout clothes, and he'd probably realized what a mistake he'd made now he was sober in the cold light of day.

I can assure you that nothing like that will ever happen again.

Getting dumped before things had even started felt pretty crappy, that was for sure.

"Earth to Kiera?" said Peach. "Are we doing this thing or not?"

Kiera looked at the bottles of bubble bath all lined up on the table in front of them. They were meant to be brainstorming her business. Figuring out a way to turn things around, to finally make a profit.

Problem was, Kiera was finding it hard to concentrate. Every time she tried to focus, she remembered the feeling of ice on her clit, and her brain started to melt...

Then her heart started to break...

"Sorry," said Kiera. "Just finding it hard to get back into the real world."

"How about we get back to basics?" Peach said, glancing over at her Shih Tzu, Teddy, who was sleeping in the corner, making a cute snoring sound. "What do you love about bubble bath?"

"Er... I just love making things clean, I guess," said Kiera.

Kiera's place was spotless, except for the bits that were impossible to clean. There was black mold on the walls which kept growing back no matter how hard she scrubbed. A rusty sink. A dangerous-looking gas stove. Kiera's old place in Connecticut hadn't been amazing, but it was a hundred times better than this. Still, at least she had a roof over her head. She knew better than anyone how much worse it would be to have no roof at all.

"Okay, that's a good start," said Peach. "But you have to be more specific than that. What, for example, do you love about your favorite products? What about this one?" She held up a bottle of 'Sparkle Splash.' It smelled like sherbet and rain.

"I guess... it makes me feel more confident," said Kiera. "It makes me feel younger, even. Full of life and possibility." She forced herself to meet Peach's gaze. "Okay, I guess I like the way it makes me feel."

"Bingo," said Peach. "That's how it makes me feel too. We'll get this bubble bath on the supermarket shelves and make you a fortune. How does that sound?" She beamed.

"It sounds like a plan," said Kiera. "But how do we do it?"

"Hmmm. That part I'm not sure about," said Peach. "I'm not much of a marketing expert. We probably need to speak to someone who *is*. Someone like... Bastion."

Kiera's stomach lurched. "No. No way. I'm not letting that man run my business."

I'm not risking having that man dump me a second time.

"Come on," said Peach. "You need this. Your lease runs out soon, and you keep refusing to take a single cent from me—"

"I didn't earn it."

"You're one of my best friends," Peach said, exasperated. "Look at this place, Kiera. It's full of mold. Actual mold. I wish you'd let me help you. Isaac and I have a whole mansion that's just sitting there empty."

Kiera scowled. "I don't accept charity."

Peach gave her a pained look. "There are times when you kinda *need* to, Kiera. You know that. You're too proud. Come on, take down some of those barriers, and let me help you."

Kiera stayed silent.

"Barriers won't always protect you, you know," Peach continued. "Come on. Just for a few weeks. Until you get back on your feet. Isaac's amazing with numbers too. Maybe he can help you find the perfect price point for your products."

"It's not the price that's the problem," Kiera sighed. "It's the... everything."

"Well, look," said Kiera, "if you won't accept charity, then maybe you need to find a job. Just something temporary, to tide you over while we get the business on track."

"I don't want a job. I'm not good at anything."

Peach seemed as though she was about to protest, but just then, her cell phone started to ring.

"Isaac?" she said, picking up. "Everything okay? I'm kinda busy helping Kiera right now."

As she spoke, she absentmindedly stroked her bump. Kiera wondered what it must feel like to be her. To have her perfect man and her baby on the way. Some people just managed to get on with their life, didn't they? Not getting eaten up by fear and chaos and anxiety like Kiera was.

"You're at Bastion's?" Peach continued, her eyes widening. "I thought you were doing some admin before we head out to the ranch tomorrow."

As well as being married and pregnant and seemingly having the best sex of their lives, Peach and Isaac had also taken over a ranch together. They were still getting it all set up and ready for the animals. It sounded... hectic.

"Why are you at Bastion's, then?" Peach asked. She frowned. "Freaking out how?"

Kiera felt her cheeks burning. Was Bastion having a meltdown because of what had happened between them? Was he revealing every last sordid detail to Isaac? Would Kiera be angry with her for not telling her all about it? She did plan to at some point, just... not yet. Not until the embarrassment had died down a little.

"I see," said Peach, then she covered her cell phone and whispered to Kiera: "Bastion's place is a pigsty. He's freaking out about it. Wants Isaac to help him tidy up. Isaac says it looks like a bomb's hit it."

Kiera rolled her eyes. She imagined what Bastion's place must look like. The man was an alcoholic scarecrow, living like a horny savage.

Apparently, he wasn't always this bad. The last few months he'd been a mess due to his divorce. So now he wanted to sort his life out.

Bit late for that, thought Kiera. *You need to stop seducing girls then running off. That's what you need.*

"Sounds like too big of a job for you, Isaac," Peach said back into her phone. "What Bastion needs is a professional cleaner."

Suddenly, she looked at Kiera. There was such determination in her eyes that Kiera could almost hear the gears whirring in her pretty little head.

Peach whispered in her ear: "You can do it. You can clean his place."

"No," said Kiera. "No way."

Just then, an alert went off on Kiera's phone.

"What was that?" Peach asked.

"It's an alarm I set to go off when my rent's three days overdue," Kiera said with a sigh.

Peach looked at her sternly. "Take the job, Kiera."

Kiera screwed her eyes tight shut. "I can't. I won't. Never."

Chapter Four

BASTION

Bastion opened the door, blinking at Kiera in disbelief.

Even though he knew she'd offered to take the cleaning job, it still felt unreal. He thought she hated him. He thought she would want to run a million miles.

"Kiera," he said, trying to keep his voice professional, "it's great to see you again."

He meant it too. It *was* great to see her. Her orange playsuit was cut tight around her curves and the blue streak in her hair looked recently dyed, lighting up in the early evening light. The swallow tattoo on her ankle was on display and the open-toe of her sandals showed her blue-painted toenails. She gave off the air of someone who liked to walk barefoot on the beach in springtime, young and carefree. She looked... like Bastion's opposite.

"Yeah, well, I need the money," said Kiera, nervously wringing her hands and following him inside. "But it's only temporary. Just while I get my business sorted."

"Of course," said Bastion stiffly. "Anything you can do to help out is fine by me."

He began showing her around his Miami mansion. The place was a mess. Empty food packets and alcohol bottles and trash everywhere. But beneath the mess, there was a minimalist masterpiece, and he looked forward to restoring the place to its former beauty.

"Wow," said Kiera, looking around wide-eyed. "This place is enormous."

She walked into the mansion's main hall with its black and white marble floors and turned briefly to look back at the view: the prawn-pink Miami skyline. Not the Scottish Highlands, that was for sure, but attractive in its own right. The soft glow of the setting sun was reflected in the many glass surfaces of the mansion's interior. Bastion felt proud to be showing Kiera his home, in spite of the mess.

Kiera stopped to look up at the large staircase. The handrail was made of oak but the sides were all glass. She ran her hand over the banister, which at first glance looked smooth, but on closer inspection was scuffed and lined. Lives had been lived here. Bastion's life. He wondered what she made of it all.

"As you can see, everything needs a good polish," he told her. "But more than that. It needs a deep clean."

"It sure does," Kiera replied, running her eyes over the worst parts of the hall, the parts full of dirty shoes and stacked-up pizza boxes. "It's going to be hard work, but it's going to be *so satisfying*."

Bastion laughed. "You really love cleaning that much?"

Kiera nodded seriously. "It's... kind of an addiction for me."

"There are worse things to be addicted to," Bastion said, his lips feeling suddenly dry. He hadn't had a drink since Scotland, though the temptation had been there. It was going to be harder than ever this evening, having *her* around the house.

He was going to have to stay strong, in more ways than one.

"Tonight we'll get the contract signed," said Bastion. "And you can stay for dinner after if you like."

"The contract?" Kiera asked, looking unnerved.

"Of course," said Bastion. "The cleaning contract."

Not the same thing as a BDSM contract.

Though I'd love to be signing one of those with you.

Kiera pouted. "You mean I don't get to start cleaning today?"

Bastion tried not to stare at her pouting lip. At that little silver ring in the middle of her lower lip, which had so often kept him awake at night as he wondered how it would feel against the smooth skin of his cock.

"You can do an hour after dinner if you like," he said, "but no working past nine. And you'll be paid for your work, obviously."

Kiera smiled. "Okay. Good. I can't bear to leave a messy place untouched."

Trying not to take offense at that, Bastion led Kiera through to his kitchen.

"We'll sign the contract here," he said.

He looked around the kitchen for a spot clean enough to go through the contract. He took in the granite worktops, covered in grease and crumbs, and the frosted glass cabinets smeared with the mess of going months without a cleaner.

His ex-wife had taken care of all that stuff: the running of the household. Not because he'd made her do it or was sexist or anything. She just liked to be in control of it. Told Bastion it was her domain and he was to keep out of it. He'd happily obliged, but in doing so he'd never really kept track of how to take care of a home. Or at least, he'd always been too busy drinking until now to take responsibility for it.

Bastion watched Kiera as she eyed the space, the kitchen looking no doubt looking even worse to her eyes. She started toward the sink, eager to get to work, but Bastion caught her by the elbow, stopping her in her tracks.

"The contract first," he said.

His heart raced as he touched her. He was reminded of how smooth her skin had felt last time he'd touched her. How responsive she was. How much he'd craved her.

He took her over to the table, wiped it with his sweater sleeve to remove the worst of the mess, and then placed down a contract he'd freshly printed off earlier and left on the countertop. This wasn't the type of contract he had dreamed of giving to Kiera, of course. This was a plain old cleaning contract, and he'd had to be careful to restrain himself in its wording.

He pushed it over toward Kiera, along with a pen, and she sat down, resting her chin on her right hand.

She turned the contract over in her hands. "What about this bit here?" she asked. "The bit about being punished if I break any of the rules?"

He paused. "Well, I have very strict expectations about how many hours you work, the quality of the work that is done, and so on. If you don't follow those rules, a punishment will be given accordingly."

Kiera frowned. "Is that standard practice?"

"It's standard when we're in my home," said Bastion firmly. He tried not to look at the way her breasts jutted out from the top of her playsuit. He tried to think of professional punishments that he could give her. Things that didn't cross a line. Things like...

His mind immediately crossed the line.

"And I really need to wear a special outfit that you choose for me?" asked Kiera.

"Of course," said Bastion. "Don't want you ruining your clothes in my home. I'll find you something that's practical but fun, I promise."

"Hmmm. Well, okay," said Kiera. "I guess I'll sign. The pay is good, anyway. That's the main thing."

She really couldn't argue with that. Bastion was paying her double what a cleaner would normally get. Plus, she didn't know it yet but he was paying for her to stay in a luxury hotel near his house. For one thing, he wanted her commute to work to be as painless as possible. For another, he'd heard from Isaac that her place was falling apart. And apparently, her lease was almost up. Bastion wasn't able to please the girl in any other way, but at least he would be able to improve her life a little.

Finally, Kiera picked up the pen, scribbling over the page with a flourish. He noticed the little heart she put for the dot of the 'i' and tried not to read anything into it. It was her signature, for heaven's sake. Not some kind of coded message.

"Great," said Bastion. "Now it's time for dinner."

Kiera looked around the kitchen. "I can't smell anything cooking."

Bastion checked his watch and then motioned toward the front door. As if by magic, the doorbell rang.

"Ooh, you ordered pizza? Well, I was going to say you didn't need to cook for me, but if it's a pizza delivery…"

Bastion gave her a mysterious half-smile then went to the door, returning with two white bags with Japanese script on them.

"Uh oh," said Kiera. "Not pizza."

"Better than pizza," Bastion told her. "Japanese food."

Kiera nervously laughed. "You know, I don't think I've even tried Japanese food. Daisy keeps raving about this food stall in the open-air market, but every time I go there, I see the hot dogs, and I just… go for what I know."

As he started taking the food out of the paper bags, he got the sense that Kiera was even more anxious than he was.

"You know, they do the best hot dogs at that place, for only two dollars," she rambled. "And sometimes, if you go at the end of the day, they literally *give them away*. If I ever end up homeless..." Kiera trailed off mid-sentence. She fiddled with her hands awkwardly.

Should he try to clear the air again? Or was the fact that she'd agreed to this job enough of a sign that she was okay with being around him?

"I have to say, I didn't think you'd want to take this job," he said. "I thought about asking you because I know that you've been going through a tough time lately—"

"Wait, who told you that?" Kiera asked spikily.

"It's written all over your face, Kiera," he gently said. "I see it all the time."

Kiera softened. "You do?"

"Sure I do. But maybe only because I've been there, too."

Kiera's cheeks blushed a cute shade of pink. "Ah yes."

"Anyway," said Bastion, steering the conversation back on track, "I'm glad you took the job. I see no good reason why the two of us can't be adults about what happened. And you'll be glad to know I've given up the drink."

"Seriously? You? Bastion Barclay? Sober as a judge?" Kiera raised an eyebrow.

"Mmm-hmm," Bastion replied, opening lids on the various food items he'd bought: katsu curry, vegetable gyoza, fried tofu, edamame beans, yakisoba. It all smelled so good. Reminded him of all the business trips he'd taken to Tokyo. Man, he had lived a full life. It was only right that he put the brakes on a little now. Let someone else have their turn.

"I, uh, I don't know how to eat with these," said Kiera, picking up a pair of wooden chopsticks and pulling them apart.

"I'll teach you," said Bastion. "I know you'll be able to pick it up. Now just watch me and copy what I do."

He held his chopsticks in the correct pose and Kiera tried to copy him.

Bastion watched her concentrate. He loved the way her eyebrows furrowed as she focused on holding the little wooden sticks. The way she dropped her food into that pretty pink mouth and then closed her eyes, as if to better feel the texture of the food between her teeth. The way those cheek dimples came out to play as she chewed.

He watched the beautiful little goddess in front of him, and he wanted her so damn bad. He wanted to pick her up from the chair and wrap her legs around his back. He wanted to hold her aloft, then throw her down on the table and eat her out in the middle of the kitchen, not caring about the state of either of them, just wanting to taste her, to make her come, and then to fill her up with himself, nestling inside her until he forgot every bad thing that had ever happened.

Most of all, he wanted to be her Daddy.

"I feel like my hands are shaking too much," said Kiera. "I'm scared of spilling noodles all over the glass table." She reached for her tumbler of water, but instantly knocked it over and the glass smashed on the marble floor. "Oh no!"

Bastion leaped up. "No matter. Seriously. I guess there is a lot of glass to smash in here."

"Yeah, no kidding," said Kiera shyly. "Everything in here is made of glass."

"Here, I have an idea."

Bastion went over to a very high-up cupboard in the kitchen and pulled down a sippy cup. His ex-wife, Pauline, had always kept a load of kids' stuff around for when visitors with young children came over. It felt a bit weird to be giving Kiera this. If he was her Daddy he'd get her a proper set of her very own. One with 'Princess' written on it or a cute picture. But this would have to do for now.

"Is that what I think it is?" asked Kiera. "A sippy cup?"

Bastion rinsed out the cup, then filled it with water. "You're a Little, aren't you?"

"Well, kinda..." Kiera said. "More of a Middle, really."

Bastion thrust the cup out to her and she took it hesitantly.

"I guess it's best not to risk breaking another glass..."

Bastion swept up the glass while Kiera ate, and he had to force himself not to hum a happy tune as he worked. It felt so good to have a woman back in the house. A *good* woman at that. Someone to care for and clean up after.

"I guess I'm not that hungry," said Kiera, putting down her chopsticks. "I should probably just get to work and then go home."

"You're not going home tonight," Bastion told her.

Kiera froze. "What do you mean?"

"I'm covering your stay at the Fairmont."

"The luxury hotel down the block?"

"I want you close by," said Bastion. "You can live there for as long as you work for me."

"But... all my stuff is at my place..."

He'd finished clearing up the glass and sat back down opposite her. "My driver will bring it to you if you like. Or keep it in storage. Whatever works best for you."

Kiera blinked at him. "I can't accept charity. This is already too much. The pay is so high. The hotel will cost a fortune."

Bastion smiled. "Not if you know the folks who run it."

"You do?" asked Kiera.

"I know the folks who run a lot of the places around here, babygirl," said Bastion.

Oops.

That final word had just slipped out.

Kiera bit her lip. "Well... alright then. It suits me really, because I have to leave my apartment soon. I decided it wasn't quite the right fit for me."

Bastion knew the true story from Isaac, which Peach had told him. Kiera couldn't afford her rent, poor girl, but he wasn't going to show her up by letting her know he knew that.

"Works for both of us, then," said Bastion. "Now listen, if you're not eating then you're welcome to go clean. You look exhausted, though. Are you sure you're up to it?"

Kiera nodded, a serious look on her face. "I'm a hard worker."

"Not too hard, I hope," said Bastion. "I prefer my staff to be well-rested."

Kiera smiled.

Bastion showed her where the cleaning products were, and Kiera got to work in the kitchen while Bastion finished his food and fired off some work emails on his phone.

It was difficult to concentrate, though. He couldn't help but take surreptitious glances at her.

He spied her bending over to clean something. Saw her cute behind wiggle as she attacked the stubborn stains on the countertop. His throat went dry, and his palms grew sweaty.

The urge to go and touch her bubbled up inside him, but he held back. It wouldn't do for a boss to get too close to his staff, no matter how hot she was. He felt like a schoolboy with a secret crush. He had to force himself to put the brakes on any thoughts of taking things further than friendship and professional courtesy allowed.

Even if his crotch *was* throbbing again...

Chapter Five

KIERA

E VERYTHING IN THE HOTEL room was magnificent, but the most magnificent thing of all was the bath.

Kiera sank farther down into the hot bath, feeling the soothing warmth of the water as it enveloped her. Then, she closed her eyes, feeling the stress of the day start to melt away.

"I could get used to this," she sighed.

She had never taken a bubble bath as luxurious as this before. The water glowed like the aurora borealis, a vibrant pattern of colors dancing across the bubbles. As well as mood lighting, the bath had gentle jets, which massaged her aching muscles. Steam rose from the surface of the water, making the room hazy and delicious.

With each breath, Kiera took in scents of cola and strawberry: a fizzy, exciting aroma that filled the air. The bubble bath was one of her own products, of course. It had been such a long time since she'd used her own stuff. Her old apartment didn't have a bathtub. The shower barely even worked. She had spent so much time thinking about how to sell her products that she had forgotten how good it felt to *use* them.

Her mind began to wander as she relaxed deeper and deeper. She thought of her trip to Scotland. The smell of the heather and pine. Maybe she could make a Scottish-inspired scent?

She thought about Miami Beach, too, about the smell of the ocean and suncream. That would make a great scent, too.

She thought about the scents of Connecticut, where she'd grown up. Apple cider donuts in the fall. Connecticut-style strawberry shortcakes, filled with whipped cream and fresh strawberries. Lemon ricotta pancakes. Sticky cinnamon buns. There were so many options.

Kiera had forgotten about this. How inspired she could feel if she gave herself the time and space to relax. She felt like herself again, even though she'd never been in a place this amazing in her whole life.

See, the thing about this hotel, the Fairmont, wasn't *just* that it was a luxury hotel. It was a luxury hotel with a secret Little suite on the top floor.

Take this bathroom, for instance. One of the taps let out soda, which made her bath extra bubbly. The walls were painted candy-pink and there were bath crayons she could draw with on the side of the beautiful ceramic tub.

Even though Bastion had insisted that having her stay at the Fairmont was in his best interest, she still felt kinda guilty about it. It was hard to accept that she deserved all this luxury and fun. But she had been exhausted after so many sleepless nights in her noisy, uncomfortable apartment that she had agreed to the gesture. And the bubble bath had been her first port of call.

"Oh boy," she said aloud, sighing deeply. "This place is heaven."

Obviously, now that she had a job, that meant that she could probably talk her landlord around to waiting a few more days for the rent. But the thought of going back there, even just to talk to him, after experiencing this was.... less than inviting.

Was there any way she could take Bastion up on his offer and just move in here for the time being?

Surely not.

Kiera tried to focus on the present. Her skin felt alive with tiny, popping bubbles. Her bubble bath, Fizz Pop, came in a powder — the kind of stuff bath bombs were made of. That made it extra fizzy in the water, and its gentle effervescence made a lovely relaxing sound. "I should probably get out soon, though," Kiera said to herself. "I need to get a good night's sleep. Work starts at seven, and Bastion told me I had to be tucked in bed by ten at the very latest."

The contract had been extremely specific about that. Work hours. Sleep hours. It had seemed a little over the top, but then Kiera had never really had a proper job with proper paperwork before, so maybe this was how things were done.

It did feel kinda good to be given rules, though. Bastion wasn't her Daddy, and he had made it very clear that he didn't want to be. But there was something very dominating about his behavior with her, and something very... Daddyish. He seemed to enjoy regressing her, even though he didn't feel like... undressing her.

Kiera reluctantly opened her eyes and slowly got out of the bath, begrudgingly leaving the warmth and comfort of the water behind. She wrapped herself in an almost ludicrously fluffy towel and padded into the bedroom.

"Jeez," she said, amazed again by how incredible the bedroom was. "How did I end up here?"

There was oversized antique furniture that looked cute but classy, and there was a large box of toys — the kind you would find in an old attic, filled with treasures. The large bed had rails like a cot, and sheets made of Egyptian brushed cotton designed to be perfectly soft against her skin.

As Kiera had told Bastion, she always saw herself as more of a Middle than a Little. She enjoyed video games, magazines, and sarcasm. Aged around fifteen if she had to put a number on it. But it was fun to be in a room like this anyway. She felt like a kid at Christmas time, wanting to run around and look at everything.

But that would have to wait. She was tired and needed to rest. She toweled off and donned the fancy new pajamas that Bastion had bought for her. Apparently, fancy pajamas were mandatory in a hotel of this caliber in case she decided to order room service in the night. She had to look stylish at all times, he'd joked. She had to admit, they were comfortable and stylish, made of baby pink satin with little hearts sewn onto the pockets. Much cuter than anything she'd normally wear, but oh-so-comfortable.

As Kiera sat on the bed, she picked up the coloring-in book that Bastion had given to her before she'd left his house — something to do in case she got lonely in a new place, he'd said.

Kiera glanced at the clock. Quarter to ten. That was okay. She could do a bit of coloring. Why not? She took the crayons out of their small, neat packet and began coloring in.

Pretty soon, Kiera found herself in what she referred to as her Little Space. Even though she never felt like the most *littley* Little, when she got into Little Space, she felt small and free, young and happy. Something she hadn't experienced in a long time. Not since she, Daisy, and Peach had all lived in Connecticut. Before men, money, and Miami.

Kiera hummed contentedly as she filled in the lines, feeling as if she was soaring on a cloud. She felt a million miles away, and could have colored for hours, but she was interrupted by the buzzing of an alarm on her phone. Bastion had programmed it for her: a bedtime reminder.

"Alright, alright, Mr. Squeaky," she told the alarm, switching it off, carefully setting aside her coloring book, and then crawling under the covers.

She flicked off the bedside light, glad of the darkness and the quiet. Even so, her brain was still buzzing.

Every time she felt herself start to drift off, Bastion's face was there, in her mind.

"I want you close by."

That's what he'd said.

She knows he didn't mean it in a sexy way, but since everything that had happened in Scotland, it was hard not to see him in a new light.

The way he had touched her in Scotland, the way he had brought her to the most intense climax of her life: it made her stomach do loop-the-loops.

Kiera let her imagination wander, picturing herself laid out on that glass table for her new boss, like a dish. She felt her body heat up as the images lingered in her mind, and before she knew it, she was lost in the throes of pleasure.

Chapter Six

BASTION

B ASTION ARRIVED HOME LATE from work. It had been a long and stressful day, and he had felt tempted to pick up a drink on the way home to help him unwind. Giving up alcohol had been surprisingly hard. He'd never quite realized just how fucking dependent he was. Since quitting drinking, he'd had tremors, restless sleep, and night sweats. But he had refused to give in to his vices. He had even taken a quick look at the photograph on his phone as he had wavered. That image of Scotland. That memory of guilt and determination to change.

But of course, remembering Scotland meant remembering... other things. Things which his fingers still remembered very well indeed.

As he opened the front door, expecting to be met with a messy mansion and a depressing night ahead of him, he was met with a pleasant surprise. The lights were on. The mess that had occupied his entrance hall just yesterday was now largely gone. In its place was some semblance of order. There were maybe ten trash bags all lined up neatly against the wall. While it wasn't sparkling in here yet, it was damn tidy compared to how it had been before. The floors were swept, the surfaces had been wiped down, and there was even the delicious smell of food cooking in the oven.

Wait… did that mean she was home?

"Kiera?" he called out. "Are you still here?"

Please be still here.

I want to see you.

Kiera appeared, standing in the middle of the hall like a vision. She was wearing the special outfit that he had bought for her to clean in. It was a cute little maid outfit with teddies on the skirt, a pink bow in her hair, and a matching pink feather duster. She looked adorable and sexy, but Bastion could also tell that she was completely wiped out.

"Kiera, sweetheart. Have you been working all day?"

Kiera smiled sheepishly. "I won't always work such long days. But I got kinda carried away today. There was so much to do, and it was so satisfying sorting it all out. I even put some food in the oven for you. Figured you could use a home-cooked meal—"

"Stay," Bastion urged her, "for dinner. With me."

Kiera looked down at her outfit and sighed. "I'm a mess."

"That's okay," he told her. "We can change you."

Kiera wiped the hair from her eyes, leaving a smear of dirt on her nose.

"You can take a shower too," said Bastion, "while I sort dinner."

Kiera nodded gratefully, perhaps too tired to argue with him. He led her upstairs to a room he'd never taken anyone into. Even his ex-wife had never been in here. He'd shown the room to Pauline once, but she had only stood at the threshold, taken one look, and then slammed the door shut.

"This is a special place," he told her outside the door, his heart racing. "It might be a little shocking for you to discover that I have a room like this, but I can assure you that you are the first person to enter it."

Kiera nodded, bemused, and Bastion took his keychain out of his pocket, locating a small gold key with a heart on it. He opened the door, then pushed it open anxiously.

"Oh wow," said Kiera, stepping into the room. "You have an adult nursery in here?"

"I built it a year ago," said Bastion awkwardly. "It was meant to be an attempt at showing my wife who I really was, but..." He ran his hand through his hair. "Anyway, never mind about her. She's not... well, she's not you."

Kiera turned back to look at him for a moment, her brown eyes both curious and exhausted. Then, she looked back at the room. "Well. I like it. Although it seems kinda... young?"

Bastion felt a stab of dejection. Did she really like it? Was she judging him?

Kiera pointed at some of the details. The little yellow ducks on the wallpaper border around the room. The mobile of clouds and stars. The cot and changing mat and stack of fresh diapers. "Do you like to regress your Littles all the way back?" she asked.

Bastion gritted his teeth together. He hoped he wasn't making a terrible mistake. He just had the feeling that Kiera was benefiting from being around a Daddy such as himself. Even if he wasn't *her* Daddy.

"Not necessarily," he replied defensively. "Although I do think there's something to be said for pushing yourself out of your comfort zone. I always thought four or five was a good age. What about you?"

Kiera shrugged. "I guess I was pretty happy back then." She paused. "But honestly, I'm not so much into all that giggly, girly stuff. Always saw my Little as more like thirteen or fourteen."

Bastion raised an eyebrow. "You sure?"

He didn't want to push the issue, but he had a feeling about Kiera. Like she was desperate to go back, *right* back, but didn't dare. He wished desperately that he could be the one to help her, but he knew that it wasn't possible. He'd try to keep things light and breezy.

"Pick out a onesie for yourself from the closet," he told her, "then go into the bathroom to shower. I'll finish off the dinner and see you down there."

"There's not a lot to finish off," said Kiera. "The lasagna is in the oven and I've already done the washing up. But you can set the table." She smiled the sweetest smile, those huge dimples appearing in her cheeks, and Bastion's heart melted.

"I'll see you downstairs, babygirl," he told her.

Oops. There he was, using that word again.

Control yourself, Bastion, he said to himself. *She's not interested in you. Not now. Not ever.*

With that, he left the room, trying to focus on the food he was about to eat. Not the girl. Anything but the girl.

*

The lasagna was perfect. Kiera knew how to combine flavors. Delicately spicy with a hint of rosemary and garlic. Tender beef with tangy cheese that brought the whole dish together. How she'd had time to do this *and* get so much cleaning done was mind-boggling. He hoped she wasn't overworking herself.

"This is so good, sweetheart," he said, taking a sip of water. "You don't need to cook me a meal every day, or in fact any day, but I appreciate this gesture."

Kiera smiled. Those dimples again. Holy fuck, those dimples. "You know, I really didn't want to take this job at first," she said. "I don't want to lose track of my bubble bath business and I wasn't sure about, you know... us. Where we stand."

Bastion nodded."I get that. What happened in Scotland between us was... intense."

Kiera blushed.

"But I want you to know that I have nothing but good feelings for you," said Bastion. "That's one of the reasons we always wound up arguing in the past. I kept putting my foot in it around you because I wanted so much to impress you."

Kiera frowned. "You, Bastion Barclay, billionaire businessman and entrepreneur, wanted to impress me — basically a nobody?"

Bastion laughed. "Yes. I, Bastion Barclay, graying old grump, wanted to impress Kiera Stark: beautiful, feisty, up-and-coming businesswoman and entrepreneur."

Kiera shifted in her seat. Her cheeks were crimson now. "Yeah. Well. Business isn't booming right now."

"It will," Bastion told her. "I believe in you."

Was he going too far? Was he making her uncomfortable? He hoped not. That was the opposite of what he was trying to do.

He focused on his food, trying not to steal too many glances at Kiera as he ate. She looked so damn adorable in the onesie she'd chosen. A leopard print that looked just right on her: wild and cute, all at once. Shame he didn't have a camel onesie. Although something told him she'd never pick it out if he did.

Kiera drank milk from her sippy cup. He'd bought a new one, especially for her. It was blue, like her hair, and it said 'Princess' on it. She was so tired, though, that she'd hardly noticed it. Her eyes grew heavy as she sipped. He had to admit that the sight of her brought a tenderness to his heart he had not felt in a long time.

Her exhaustion was palpable. She yawned and said, "Sleepy now."

He smiled at her and said, "You can stay here if you like."

She looked up at him, her eyes widening in surprise. "But the expensive hotel room..."

He waved his hand in dismissal. "It's no problem. You can barely keep your eyes open. I have plenty of space for you here."

Kiera yawned. "Thank you, sir."

In response, he scooped her up in his arms and carried her upstairs to the nursery. She felt so light as he held her. Maybe he wasn't as old and worn-out as he sometimes thought. He was only in his late forties, after all. There was life in him yet!

He took her into the nursery bathroom and found a new toothbrush in the cupboard. He chose a baby blue one with cartoon monkeys on it. Another possible spirit animal for Kiera. Monkeys were social, confident, playful, creative, and rebellious. He'd have told Kiera why he picked it, but she looked too tired to converse. She simply sat on his lap while he perched on the edge of the bath, and then she opened her mouth wide for him.

"Good girl," he said, cleaning her teeth. "It's important we keep up your oral hygiene, even when you're as tired as this."

Kiera made a small noise of agreement, nestling against his shoulder. Man, the feeling of her warm body pressing down on his. It felt almost like his dick was...

Stop it, Bastion. You're only going to disappoint yourself.

He carried her through to the bedroom and laid her down on the adult-sized cot then tucked her in, lifting up the side rails so she didn't fall out of the unfamiliar bed.

She curled up on her side and looked up at him, blinking. "Like it here."

Bastion carefully tucked a strand of hair behind her ear and kissed her forehead. "Do you need anything, babygirl? Water? A bedtime story?"

Kiera shook her head. "Need sleep. Little bit hot."

"You want me to crack open a window?"

Kiera closed her eyes, too tired to answer, but her slender hands unzipped her onesie, and her bare breasts were revealed to him, gleaming in the moonlight. "Better now," she said.

Bastion felt *himself* blush for once.

"Um. G-goodnight," he stammered.

"Na-night, Daddy," Kiera said with a small sigh.

For a moment, Bastion was lost in the sight of her pert breasts, mesmerized by the curve of her nipples and the way they puckered in the cool air. He felt a stirring in his groin but quickly dismissed it.

Stop this, Bastion.

Embarrassed, he turned away from Kiera and swiftly left the room. He stumbled down the hallway, his heart racing as he struggled to keep his thoughts under control.

She called me Daddy.

She showed me her breasts.

She let me dominate her.

Finally, unable to resist the urge any longer, he slipped his hand into his pants and began to stroke himself.

Suddenly, with an irresistible, primal force, like lava rising up from a volcano, Bastion's dick grew thick and hard. He gasped as he felt his erection grow in his palm. This wasn't just a semi. This was a full-on, rock-hard boner.

Unable to resist, he leaned against the glass staircase, pumping his cock as fast as he possibly could, groaning as he spilled what felt like bucketfuls of pent-up semen all over the reflective surface.

Damn.

Kiera Stark had made him hard.

And Kiera Stark was going to make him hard over and over again from now on. He could sense it, deep within his balls. And deep within his heart.

Chapter Seven

KIERA

K IERA WOKE UP WITH a sleepy yawn. It took a moment for her to realize where she was, but then she recognized the crib in Bastion's nursery and smiled a happy smile.

He really cares about me, she thought.

She took in her surroundings with a contented sigh, feeling the warmth and comfort of the soft bedding around her. There was a teddy beside her, pink and cheerful, with a rainbow on its tummy, and she gave it a big squeeze.

"Hello, what's your name?"

The teddy bear looked at her with unblinking eyes.

"I think I'll call you Blinky," she said, laughing.

She looked around the room now, her eyes widening with wonder at the array of toys and trinkets.

"I have to start work in half an hour," she said, checking her watch. She didn't mean to sleep so long. She must have been exhausted. "But that's okay because I'm already at work! Half an hour is long enough for a quick play, right Blinky?"

Blinky didn't blink.

She laughed again.

As she swung her legs over the side of the low cot, she noticed her onesie was unzipped. Quick as a flash, the memory returned to her: she had unzipped it in front of Bastion! She had been so tired, and felt so comfortable around him, that she had done it without thinking.

Oh jeez. What must he have thought?

She wondered, for a moment, if he had liked what he saw. Absent-mindedly, she began grinding her hips, rubbing her groin against the mattress. Wanting more, she pushed the pink bear between her legs and rubbed against that too.

Mmmmm.

She thought about how good it had felt to be looked after Bastion last night. To have him carry her up to bed. To let him clean her teeth. To unzip herself in front of him.

She slid her hand into her onesie, massaging her left breast, as she thought about what happened in Scotland.

Bastion's thick fingers on her clit.

The ice and fire between her legs.

How long he'd pushed her to the very edge of that intense—

Oh, holy f...udge.

Before she knew it, she felt the warm spread of pleasure spreading around her thighs and pooling in her tummy, sending sparks of satisfaction up to her brain.

"Oops," she said to the stuffie.

Blinky didn't seem to mind.

She zipped up her onesie and climbed out of bed, noticing a jungle puzzle made of chunky wooden pieces over by the window. A distant memory fired up in her. She'd had something like this as a kid. Maybe even this exact brand of puzzle. She held the pieces and gave them a sniff. The pieces smelled like pencil shavings.

Instantly, she was transported back to her youth. She remembered the jigsaw's smell and even its taste. She put a piece between her teeth and bit down on it. Oh yes, she remembered that feeling. Her new little baby teeth found the feeling of that chunky wood so satisfying.

She began playing with the jigsaw, singing nursery rhymes happily to herself. A lot of people said that the best way to tackle a jigsaw was to start with the corner pieces, then the edges, then start filling in the details. But those were the kind of people who weren't attracted to what was brightest and boldest. The kind of people who probably saved their favorite part of a meal until last. Kiera wasn't like that. She liked to jump right into whatever excited her most.

So, she found the pieces for the bright red flying parrot and the pouncing tiger. She was about to start work on the monkey swinging in the vine when her beeping phone interrupted her.

"Oh noooo! Work time."

At least she was already at work, but she still had to get dressed. She was meant to wear another maid's outfit. Bastion had already laid a clean one out for her. But there were so many other cute outfits in here to try. Surely he wouldn't mind if she tried something new?

She selected a cute little babydoll dress with puff sleeves and a matching baby blue ribbon for her hair. It was an *Alice in Wonderland* kind of a dress. Nothing like the sort of thing she usually wore, but then, lately, she hadn't been doing any of her usual stuff. It was kind of like she was on vacation from herself right now, and that was okay. It was actually quite thrilling.

She tied her hair back, smiling at her reflection in the mirror.

"Hello, Alice," she said, curtseying at her reflection. "Have you seen the Mad Hatter anywhere?"

Suddenly, she heard a stern voice calling for her from outside the room.

"Uh oh. That sounds like him."

She scrambled to her feet and hurried out of the room, her ponytail bobbing with every step. "I'm coming, I'm coming!" She ran down the stairs, tripping down the last steps and almost falling onto her knees, but managing to save herself at the last moment.

Bastion, her boss, stood at the bottom of the stairs, wearing a crisp black business suit, with his arms crossed. A strange look flickered in his eyes. He scrutinized her with a critical eye. Then, seeming to recover himself, he tightened his jaw as he waved a bit of paper in the air. Their contract.

"This contract stipulates that you must not be late," he told her. "We agreed that if you broke any of my rules, there would be consequences."

Kiera bit her lip and her stomach sank as he paused, letting the ramifications of her mistake sink in.

It was true that she was about fifteen minutes late, but then she had worked later than she was meant to yesterday. She had even cooked dinner for her boss. Couldn't he go easy on her?

"I... I was so tired," she said pitifully, "after all that extra work yesterday. Not taking any breaks. Making lasagna—"

"It was very thoughtful of you to go the extra mile," Bastion said, his voice softening just for a moment, "but you must not overwork yourself. Work starts at the same time every day, whether you worked extra the day before or not. Whether you skip breaks or not. The structure is in place for a reason, Kiera. It is there to help you plan and pace yourself."

Kiera bit her lip, looking up at Bastion, her eyes widening with fear. "So... you're going to punish me?"

Bastion nodded. "I'm afraid so, Little one. Not only are you late for work, but you are also wearing the wrong attire. And rules are rules, my dear. They're made in your own best interest."

Kiera wanted to ask what was so different about her wearing this dress to her maid's outfit, but she didn't want Bastion to think she was being cheeky. The last thing she needed was an even bigger punishment.

"You have a choice," Bastion continued. "The first option is that you can have your wages docked by an hour."

Instantly, Kiera shook her head. There was no way she was letting him dock her pay. She had worked so hard yesterday. She needed this money so badly. She would take the other punishment, no matter what.

"What's the other option?" she asked meekly.

"The second option is a little... spicier," he told her.

"Spicier, sir?"

"Yes," he replied authoritatively. "The second option is a spanking."

Kiera gulped, her cheeks reddening with embarrassment. She had let Bastion slap her bottom that one time in Scotland, but they had been drunk...ish.

This was different.

It was daytime.

They were both sober.

She was... into him.

Or, at least, she kept having naughty thoughts about him. Naughty thoughts that led to naughty little climaxes.

She looked up at Bastion, her heart flapping wildly in her chest. He looked back at her, his face unreadable.

"I... um... I guess I choose the spanking," she said, her voice catching in her throat.

Bastion's posture stiffened slightly. "Good," he said. "I think that option is the most appropriate."

Bastion led her down the hall to his study. She hadn't been in here before. It had been locked while she had cleaned yesterday, as a few of the rooms had been. The room was dark, lit only by the rays of weak morning sun coming in from a nearby window on one side. Shelves lined the walls and upper half of the room, stuffed full of books and papers and knick-knacks. A large glass desk sat in the middle of the room, with a leather chair behind it and another leather seat in the corner.

Bastion headed straight for the seat in the corner, then patted his lap.

"Come on," he told her. "I'm already late for work. Don't make me any later."

Kiera took a deep breath. She could handle this. Just a quick spanking from her hot older boss. The hot older boss who had given her the best orgasm of her life in Scotland. The hot older boss who she'd masturbated about this morning. Which was one of the reasons she was late and had to be spanked right now. This was fine. Everything was fine.

"Hurry up," said Bastion. "I haven't got all day."

Kiera went over to his lap, her hair still bobbing with that blue ribbon, her stomach still doing backflips.

"Good girl," he said. "Panties down now."

Kiera lifted the hem of her dress and pulled down her panties. Bastion had supplied the nursery with a bunch of cotton panties with various designs on them: ducks and bunnies and flowers. Today, she had picked out a pair with a crocodile on.

"Lie down on my lap," Bastion told her, spreading his thighs wide and indicating how she should lie on him.

She complied, her heart pounding in her chest as she awaited her punishment.

"You remember your safeword, I trust?" he told her.

"Thistle," she said quietly.

"Good," he said. "If this gets too much, or you decide that you want me to stop for whatever reason, then I'll stop. Your wages will not be docked and there will be no further punishment. You understand?"

Kiera wondered if she should just stop this right now if her wages wouldn't be docked. But something inside her knew that this was what she *wanted*. She wanted to feel his strong palm on her butt cheeks again. She wanted to take whatever Bastion wanted to give her. Over and over again.

"Ten smacks," he told her. "Five for being late and five for wearing the wrong outfit."

Immediately after that, his hand came down hard on her bottom hard.

"Ow!"

The pain spread around her bottom cheeks with the intensity that the orgasm had spread around her thighs less than an hour ago. It felt different, but oddly, almost as pleasurable.

Before she had the chance to think about it anymore, another slap rained down on her. Each time, the sting gave way to a dull throbbing; intense but bearable, painful but pleasurable,

He continued spanking her, his hand coming down in a hard, steady rhythm.

Slap!

Slap!

Slap!

Tears began streaming down Kiera's face as the pain intensified. Despite her tears, she knew that this punishment was necessary. Not just because she had broken the rules. Because she *needed* this.

A sign that somebody else in this big, bad world had her own best interests at heart. He cared about what she did. He wanted to guide her, teach her, show her.

Finally, after what felt like forever, Bastion stopped spanking her. He helped Kiera off his lap and she stood there, her bottom still throbbing from the punishment.

"Your punishment is over now, Little one," he said.

She nodded, her cheeks still flushed from the spanking. She noticed that her pussy was so wet that moisture was starting to trickle down her thigh. She tried to hide it, but she must have drawn more attention to herself because Bastion's eyes flicked down.

"That turned you on, sweetheart?" he asked. "There's no need to be embarrassed."

Kiera looked down at Bastion's lap and she was *sure* that she could see a bulge in his pants. Was he as turned on as her?

"I think I need some aftercare," she whispered.

"Of course," Bastion replied right away. "I'd like to care for you very much. Would you like me to run you a bath? Give you a massage?"

She looked up at him. "No, Daddy," she whispered, remembering how much he seemed to like her calling him that last night. "I know you're running late for work now, but I was hoping we might..." She paused, anxious that she was saying too much.

Bastion stared at her. "I like it very much when you call me Daddy."

"I like calling you that," said Kiera, adding: "*Daddy*."

All her life, Kiera had thought she was some kind of punk. That her spirit animal was a sea urchin or a porcupine or a thorny dragon. Turned out that around the right man, she was a Little kitten.

Bastion moaned a low moan, then he stood up, walking forward so forcefully that Kiera had to walk backward. She fell back over his large glass desk and he hoisted her up onto it.

He pulled her thighs apart, her pussy bare and wet for him, and he pushed his face between her legs.

Kiera gasped as his lips touched her. So warm and soft and insistent. Kissing and gently biting and sucking on her velvet lips. Pushing his finger inside of her at the same time, bringing her pleasure so expertly it was as though he knew her body inside out.

"Oh, Daddy…" she moaned. "I can hardly…"

"Then don't hold back," he urged her. "Just come. As hard as you like."

The last time he had made her climax, he had held her at the very edge of that precipice for as long as was humanly possible. This time, though, he was letting her leap right off, plummeting into the quickest, fastest, most electric orgasm of her life.

She pushed her bare, stinging ass down into the cold glass desk as her body trembled and shook, and felt like it was shattering into a million tiny pieces.

Bastion looked down at her, his eyes fixed on hers. His expression was the most serious she had ever seen it.

"Stay here again tonight," he told her. "In fact, screw it. Move in here." It sounded like an order.

"Yes, Daddy," she said, her head spinning. "I'll do it."

Chapter Eight

BASTION

BASTION WAS STUCK IN an important meeting when his phone buzzed. It was an incoming picture message.

Against his better judgment, he glanced at the screen under his desk and saw a photo of Kiera, showing a close-up of her pert, delicious butt to the camera as it glowed red from the morning's recent spanking. "I can see your handprint on my bottom!" said the text accompanying the picture.

Bastion felt his heart skip a beat and his hands clench into fists. How was he supposed to concentrate on the meeting now? He forced himself to look away from the message and tried to focus on the conversation.

But no matter how hard he tried, he couldn't help but think of Kiera's bottom, the memory of her body beneath his hands, and the way she sighed with pleasure as the punishment was dealt.

Plus, the taste of her deliciously sweet pussy. Like candy canes and bubble baths and... sex.

The intensity of his desire was almost too much to bear. His cock was straining to get out of his pants. He had to get out of there.

"I'm sorry," he said abruptly, standing up, hiding his crotch with some paperwork. "I have to go."

His client — the owner of a string of exclusive beach huts over at Bal Harbor — looked surprised. Isaac, who was attending the meeting remotely from his ranch, looked pissed. But Bastion didn't give either of them a chance to object. He rushed out of the room, his heart pounding. He had been struggling with his impotence for many months, but now, his body seemed to have come alive again. He had to take care of himself before he returned.

He made his way to the bathroom, and when he was safely locked inside, he quickly unzipped his pants. He ran his hands over his already thickening cock, shivering with anticipation. He thought of Kiera and began to stroke himself, the pleasure intensifying with every passing second.

Last night's hard-on had been a revelation. Allowing himself to come outside Kiera's room like that had been exciting and unexpected. But almost as soon as the deed was done, he'd gotten hard again. He'd spent the night stroking boner after boner into submission, thinking of Kiera's gorgeous body and cute dimples, and he'd come so many times he'd lost count.

And then this morning...

This morning, the spanking had been unexpected. But he had given Kiera the choice to be spanked because he wanted to see if it was what *she* wanted. He knew how much she'd enjoyed it when he'd spanked her in Scotland, and he sensed that there was something deeper between them.

Obviously, he'd been right. She *had* wanted the spanking. Even when he told her that she wouldn't really lose any of her wages. It was important that she knew that. He wasn't there to bribe or blackmail her. He wanted to be a fair boss. He wanted that with all his might. But clearly, they both had feelings developing. Feelings he'd be an idiot not to explore.

And man, he was going to explore them.

He was going to explore the *hell* out of them.

He stroked himself faster now, as he looked at the photograph of Kiera's beautiful reddened ass. His dick begged him to go faster and faster, it begged him to imagine what it would feel like squeezing between those cheeks, finding her tight little hole, and filling it up with his girth.

Hot fucking damn...

He came into a thick wad of toilet tissue, panting with relief. He quickly cleaned himself up and then he fired off a quick message to Kiera. "No more naughty texts when Daddy's at work," he told her. Then, in case that was too cold, he added: "Daddy's dick can't take it."

As soon as he hit send, he hoped it wasn't too much. Kiera had agreed to move in with him, but under what conditions? They needed to define their relationship, and that was exactly what he would do tonight.

Crazy as it had been to ask her to move in, he knew that it was right. He needed to keep Kiera close to him right now. Obviously, there was a sexual side to this. He wanted to make her come like he had done this morning over and over again. He wanted to make sure the woman who had cured his cock barely left his sight ever again.

But there was more to it than that.

Kiera was a precious jewel in need of his protection. He couldn't bear the thought of her alone in a hotel, without a proper home. He needed to help her with her business. He'd been desperate to offer her his aid with it, but wanted to take his time, so it didn't seem patronizing. Whenever she felt ready, though, he wanted to help Kiera get her life exactly where she wanted it to be.

If she wanted it to be with him, then so much the better.

If she didn't... well, she was free to leave at any time.

His phone buzzed as a new message from Kiera came in. "Sorry, Daddy. I will let you instigate things between us when you feel it is a good time. You're the boss."

He liked that. *You're the boss*. Spoke to his dominant side. Damn, it felt good to have a submissive in his life. His ex-wife had been very far from submissive. She had just been... chaotic, like him. That's the reason it used to work between them. Until she fell pregnant by accident, and then Bastion tried to sort himself out, but she didn't. The whole thing had been a mess.

Ah well.

Fuck it.

He had a beautiful Little waiting at home who was getting to know the new Bastion — the Bastion that didn't use alcohol as a crutch and was learning to be a good man.

He left the bathroom and felt his phone buzz again. This time it was Isaac, who had obviously just finished the meeting without him.

"What was that about, man?" Isaac asked. "Did you go and jerk off in the office bathroom again?"

"Uh, yeah," said Bastion. "I guess I did." Now that he was telling the truth about that, it felt way more embarrassing to admit to it.

"Next time, wait until the meeting is over," Isaac warned him. "We almost lost the beach hut deal."

"You did?" Bastion felt a sting of guilt.

"Don't worry. I worked my magic and wowed her with some figures," said Isaac. "We're getting a beach hut for exclusive use by Daddies Inc. Half the price she originally asked for it, too." Isaac paused. "We're going to have to trust you, though, man. Once I'm at the ranch full-time, I won't be able to attend a lot of the meetings in person. If Montague's away, like he is now, you'll be on your own."

Once Isaac and Peach's ranch was fully operational, the plan was that Isaac would attend most meetings virtually. Most of his work involved spreadsheets and computer stuff anyway. It was good that their work at Daddies Inc. allowed them all to be flexible, living out their dreams, while at the same time being committed to the job. So far, Bastion had squandered all his opportunities, but not anymore.

"You know, you need a girlfriend," Isaac told him. "Well, more than a girlfriend. You need a Little."

Bastion said nothing. He didn't want to tell anyone about Kiera just yet. After all, they hadn't even fucked. He wanted Kiera to be the one to decide when to tell people, and what to tell them.

"I think you should take a break, Bastion," continued Isaac. "You haven't really stopped working since the shit hit the fan with Pauline. Go take a break. Somewhere with Littles."

Bastion shrugged. "Nah."

"Seriously," Isaac urged him. "I hear Littlecreek Ranch is nice this time of year. Get yourself a nice little submissive and she can clean for you too. Or what about Liberty? There are some real cuties there. And if you don't mind sharing, I hear a lot of them are up for having more than one Daddy—"

Bastion raised a hand to stave off Isaac's excitable suggestions. But come to think of it, his friend had a point. He'd heard good things about Liberty. And he knew Haze too, back from when he lived the party lifestyle in New York and Haze ran the Electric Zoo. It was where he'd met his ex-wife, Pauline, as it happened.

An idea began forming in his mind. He *would* go on vacation, but he'd go with Kiera. There was no way he'd leave her behind. Maybe a vacation would be good for them.

He hurried to his office and locked the door, then he took out his phone.

It only rang one time before Kiera picked up.

"Daddy?" she asked. "Is this you instigating something?"

"How about we make this a videocall, babygirl?" he asked her. "This is your break time, and I want to check that you're relaxing."

"Uh, sure..." said Kiera, switching to a video call. Bastion was sure he saw her hiding a feather duster behind her back. She was still wearing her blue dress, too.

"Well, that's very naughty," he told her. "I told you to put your maid's outfit back on."

"Oh," she said, disappointed. "I forgot after we... I thought the punishment maybe canceled it out..."

Bastion laughed. "No, sweetheart. But Daddy wants you to change out of that outfit after we speak. That dress cost half a million dollars, and if you spill cleaning products on it—"

"Half a million dollars?" Kiera's jaw hit the floor and a look of panic spread across her face.

Bastion laughed even harder. "Got you. It wasn't that expensive. But still, the fabric of that dress is dry-clean only. We don't want to get dirt and grime all over it if we can help it. Your maid's outfit is made from tough, washable fabric. That way, we won't ruin any of your other clothes."

Kiera smiled. "Are you saying that I get to keep all the clothes in the nursery?"

"Of course, darling," Bastion said, smiling. "It's your room now. Everything in it belongs to you. Now listen, you're meant to be taking a break. You're not being a bad girl and doing extra work, are you? I don't want you crashing out on me tonight. We have things to discuss."

Kiera looked to the left and right of the screen awkwardly. "I, er, I'll start my break now, Daddy."

"Yes," said Bastion. "But first: you broke another rule. Which means you get another punishment."

"You're reducing my pay?" Kiera asked, wincing.

"No, darling. You don't have anything to worry about where your wages are concerned. It was naughty of Daddy to talk about docking your wages this morning. From now on, all your punishments will be of a... different nature. But they won't all be pleasant, so I don't want you doing naughty things on purpose."

Kiera fidgeted nervously. "So... how are you punishing me, Daddy?"

Bastion gazed at the beautiful girl on his screen. His cock twitched lustfully as he started to speak. "Go to your nursery," he told her, "and open the cabinet in your bathroom."

Kiera bit her lip. "Now?"

"Yes, sweetheart," he said. "But keep holding the phone up so that I can watch you."

Kiera obediently followed his instructions. He watched her climb the stairs, then go into the nursery. Then, he watched her expression change as she opened the bathroom cabinet.

"There's a... b-bottom plug... in here, Daddy," she stammered.

"Good girl," he reassured her. "You recognized what it is. Take it out."

Kiera appeared to reach for the item and then held it up to the camera. Next to her small face, it looked so big. It was sapphire blue, just like the streak in her hair. Back when he bought it, he never knew it would end up in his dream woman's hands. Now, he could see that it suited her perfectly. Like Cinderella's glass slipper, it was made for her.

"It's very big, Daddy," she whispered.

"It is," he replied. "But you're going to put some lubricant on it now, and then you're going to take a nice big deep breath and slide it into your asshole while Daddy watches. Do you understand?"

"Yes, Daddy," said Kiera. She rested the camera on the sink, and then let him see her apply a big dollop of lubricant to the sterile plug. "Is that enough?"

"More than enough, babygirl," he said. "That'll go in nice and easy if you do as I say."

Kiera nodded dutifully.

"Now take off all your clothes for me," he said, "then go and stand facing that far wall." He pointed at the screen.

She walked over to the wall and gave him a coy smile as she let him look at her full breasts, then she turned around and wiggled her ass for him.

Holy fuck, that ass.

"Keep facing that wall," he said, aware that his dick was thickening more and more with each passing second. "That's it. Now bend over and pull open your cheeks for me."

He watched, transfixed, as Kiera did as she was told, showing him her tight rosebud. Damn, he wished that he was right there with her, his tongue lapping at her little pink hole.

"Take a nice big deep breath in for Daddy, and then as you exhale, I want you to start pushing in the plug."

Kiera hesitated a moment, clearly building up the courage for the act, and then he watched her tight asshole start to stretch open as the bulbous glass object entered her.

Of course, he imagined that the plug was his dick. Of course, his hand started to stray inside his pants. Of course, he held his fat cock and began to stroke it as he looked at the blue plug wedged in her asshole like a huge pacifier for her butt.

"Good," he said, his voice strained. "In a moment, you're going to go and sit on my couch and wait there for me, with that butt plug nestled between your cheeks until Daddy gets home from work. Understand? I'm forcing you to take a break, babygirl. But if you do any work or take out that plug, there'll be consequences."

Kiera turned around, standing up straight and wincing for a moment as the plug repositioned itself deep inside her back passage.

"What if I get thirsty?"

"Bring your sippy cup."

"And... what if I need the bathroom?"

He flung the answer back to her without thinking. "Wear a diaper. There's a huge stack of them in the nursery."

"A diaper?" she asked uncertainly.

"Sure," he replied. "You might discover you like it. I hear they're very comforting."

Kiera paused. "What if I spot something that needs cleaning?"

"No chance."

"And... what happens when you get home?" asked Kiera quietly.

"When Daddy gets home," Bastion said, his voice catching, "then he replaces the plug with his nice thick cock."

"He does?" Kiera whispered, her hands unconsciously traveling down between her legs. He swore that even on his small phone screen he could see the wetness down there.

"You want proof?" Bastion asked.

Kiera nodded. "Yes please, Daddy."

Bastion angled the phone down to his groin and unbuttoned his fly. His cock sprung out, fully erect and lined with veins. He held its thick girth in his fist, showing her the hungry purple head of his dick.

"That plug is just making room for this," he told her, pumping his dick up and down. He held his phone farther away from himself now, so that he could look at her as she watched him.

He saw that she had gone into the nursery and was lying in her cot, rubbing the teddy bear between her thighs as she sucked on her finger and with her other hand, toyed with her breast.

"I see my babygirl is a little worked up," Bastion said.

"You look a little worked up too, Daddy," said Kiera. "Your big snake looks like it wants to do bad things to me."

"It wants to make its home in you," said Bastion. "It wants to tunnel deep inside you and live there forever."

"I want that," said Kiera. "I want that very much." She had taken her finger out of her mouth to speak, but put it back in again now, sucking on it so hard that he couldn't help imagining that it was his own dick.

"Take that finger out of your mouth," Bastion commanded her, "and rub it on your clit. The saliva will feel good. I want to watch you make yourself come."

Kiera did as she was told, lying back on her bed, and instantly started sighing.

"You're going to make Daddy come too," he told her. "You're going to make Daddy come very hard."

He couldn't believe how turned on he was, and in his office as well. He looked around his office for a good place to come. Like his home, everything in here was glass. His desk, his smoked ombre glass chair, and the huge window looking out over Miami.

Fuck it, he thought. *I've felt powerless for too long. I'm big, I'm strong, I'm hard. I'm a fucking boss.*

He stepped over to his office window, jerking off as he held his phone against it, watching Kiera's beautiful pussy grow pinker and wetter as she gave it the love it needed.

Then, as Kiera's moans grew more guttural and her legs shook more uncontrollably, Bastion couldn't hold it in any longer. He came hard and fast against the glass window.

"Shit," he panted, looking at Kiera's quivering thighs, and the satisfied smile playing across her lips. "You make me feel on top of the world, babygirl."

"You too, Daddy," said Kiera. "And I promise I'll behave until you get back."

Bastion looked at the mess he'd made on his window. At least he was so high up here, nobody would have been able to see that. But he needed to stop coming on shiny surfaces very soon. He needed to come deep within his gorgeous, soft babygirl.

Chapter Nine

KIERA

K IERA WAS STILL TRYING to wrap her head around what she had just done. Phone sex. With Bastion Barclay. While wearing the world's biggest butt plug.

It was almost too much to comprehend. She badly wanted to talk to her friends about the strong feelings she was experiencing. To work out whether the stuff she was doing with Bastion was... right or not. She had spent so long hating the man, after all, that she wanted to be reassured that she hadn't gone completely crazy. Some kind of early midlife crisis, maybe. Or perhaps the desperate dive in her business sales was leading her to make all kinds of impulsive decisions that weren't in keeping with her usual aloof self.

Normally, she was all about barriers. Protecting herself from the outside world. From all the troublesome characters in life who were about to hurt her.

With Bastion, she had well and truly let her guard down. She was following his instructions to the letter.

Now, here she was, sitting on his couch, with the plug still in her ass and the recent orgasm still making her heart pound. Despite the relief she'd experienced in her cot, the plug was making her permanently turned on. Every tiny movement she made pushed the plug into some new part of her ass. It rubbed against her pussy from the inside. It stretched her at the back and made her hungry at the front.

It felt strange to be in this constant state of arousal and yet not be able to act on it. Plus, even stranger than that, she had done something she never thought she would do – she had put on a diaper straight after the call. A diaper! She still couldn't believe it. It was a pull-up with an elasticated waistband and a picture of a chick on the front. Bastion had been right, too. It felt super comforting. Hard to explain why, really. It just felt like she was being hugged around the middle. Protected and safe from the outside world.

So now, her bottom was plugged up and wrapped in a soft, crinkly diaper, as she rubbed her crotch back and forth thinking about her boss' thick, purple-headed dick, stretching her bumhole even wider the moment he walked in through the front door.

Luckily, she was wearing the leopard print onesie. She had put it on to keep warm, but also to make extra sure that she couldn't touch herself and disobey Bastion's commands. It was zipped up all the way to the neck, hiding any trace of the naughtiness going on underneath.

It seemed amazing that the diaper wasn't even visible. Made her wonder how many other Littles there were walking around in public wearing diapers and she never even knew about it! Maybe Daisy and Peach did it too and she never knew. Maybe Daisy or Peach had even peed in her presence, secretly wetting their crinkly diapers.

Uh oh. Thinking about peeing was making her want to go to the bathroom. She had promised Bastion that she would stay on the couch, and that meant that she only had one choice if she wanted to pee. Although she had put the diaper on, she wasn't sure that she was ready to take the step of relieving herself in it.

She had to think about something else.

She sighed and looked around the living room. She hadn't expected to end up in a relationship like this, with a man like Bastion. So rich and so... in love with glass. But it just felt so good. She was still learning, though; she was discovering new things about herself and her sexuality with every passing day.

The thought of Bastion coming home and taking control of the situation excited her, but it also terrified her. He was able to bring out the naughty side of her that she hadn't even known existed. He could make her feel both powerful and vulnerable at the same time.

She hadn't made herself vulnerable in forever. It felt oddly freeing.

She couldn't let her guard down completely, though. She had to watch out. People always, always had a way of letting you down. Men weren't princes. They were dirty dogs with dirty secrets. It was only a matter of time before she discovered Bastion's.

Still, as long as she didn't become totally dependent on him, she'd be okay. She had to increase her business sales to give herself some independence. It's not like she planned on being his cleaner forever, even though she was enjoying cleaning the mansion. So many surfaces to polish. So much to make clean and shiny.

Now that she'd agreed to move in with Bastion, though, she wasn't sure how the job was going to work. Would he keep paying her? Was she... a housewife now? Expected to clean his house as part of her wifely duties?

Hold your horses, Kiera. You're not marrying the man. You're waiting for him to come home and butt-fuck you. There's a difference. A big one.

Kiera shifted on her seat. Holy fudge, she needed to pee. Looked like she was running out of options here. She could either go against Bastion's wishes and get up to go to the bathroom... or she could pee in this diaper.

If she took the first option, he might never find out. But the guilt of the lie would eat away at her, and that would be worse than him knowing the truth. She didn't want to let him down, though. She wanted to be a good girl for him. Because, quite simply, being a good girl felt good. And Bastion was maybe, just maybe, the first person in her messed-up life who had ever seen her as good.

So, she took a deep breath, and then just... let go.

She felt the wetness trickle out of her, spreading around her pussy, her butt, and the top of her thighs. She had obviously drunk way too much water earlier, but luckily the diaper was ultra-absorbent. In a matter of moments, the wetness had been sucked up by it, leaving behind nothing but a warm, tingly sensation. A pleasant reminder of how very good she had just been.

"Wow," she whispered. "That felt weirdly great. I really *must* be going crazy."

Knock knock!

Just then, she was interrupted from her thoughts by a loud knock.

Bastion!

She jumped up from her seat, bouncing over to the door, ready to tell her Daddy what she had just done.

But even as she pulled back the door, she knew that something wasn't right.

Bastion wouldn't have knocked. He had a key. This wasn't...

It was a boy.

A teenage boy, maybe thirteen or fourteen. He had spiky, gelled hair and wore a Metallica t-shirt. A bit retro, but not a bad band choice, in her opinion.

"Can I help you?" she asked, touching the zipper of her onesie, making sure she was completely covered up. She could feel the thickness of her diaper between her legs, and the weight of the butt plug sitting in her ass. This was majorly embarrassing. Why the heck had she opened the door?

The boy scowled at her. Something about those green eyes looked familiar, but she didn't know any teenage boys so she had to be mistaken.

"Great," said the teen sarcastically. "There's a freak in my house."

Kiera looked confused, her mouth agape, as the spiky teenager barged past her and into the house.

She watched him dump his bag down in the living room, not far from the couch where she'd just relieved herself in her puffy white diaper. And then, she watched him stomp upstairs, past her secret nursery, and all the way to a room at the end that she'd never entered. He took out a key and unlocked the door, then let himself inside, slamming the door behind him.

Frozen in place, Kiera's pulse quickened.

Oh my god. Bastion Barclay has a teenage son.

*

Kiera sat in the nursery wearing her normal clothes: ripped jeans and a t-shirt. She had removed the plug, obviously, as well as the wet diaper, and she was so shaken by the whole thing she had almost thrown up in the bathroom while she did it.

As she sat in her cot, hugging her teddy bear, so many thoughts ran through her mind.

Why hadn't Bastion told her about his son? Why had he instructed her to sit on his couch when his son was due home? Did the son know about this room — the nursery? Did he know that his father was a Daddy Dom? Did he know that *she* was a Little?

The shame. The embarrassment. The guilt.

She felt as though she'd never live this down.

And yet... she also felt a very, very slight feeling of relief.

She had been waiting for Bastion to slip up, and here it was. Proof that he was not perfect for her. That he was a liar and an asshole, just like everyone else.

Better to find out now than in a week or a month or a year.

From the other side of the house, loud music started playing through bassy speakers. It wasn't Metallica or a metal band, though. It was the sound of a game. A game she knew very well, in fact. It was a video game! And not just any game. It was one of Kiera's favorites: Final Fantasy Six. She listened for a moment as the melancholic tune of *Searching for Friends* sounded out through the house.

She went over to her door and peeped out, noticing that the teenage boy's door was slightly ajar now. Should she go and say something to him? Introduce herself, maybe? It's not like she could stay hiding in her nursery until Bastion came home, could she?

Maybe she should just leave. He was clearly distracted by the game. She could just pack her stuff and go right now, before Bastion even had a chance to explain what was going on.

That music, though... She had been in the middle of playing that videogame when her parents had kicked her out, leaving her homeless aged fifteen.

She had always wondered if that's why she had thought of herself as a Middle. She'd become stuck at the point when she'd been kicked out of her own life, never being allowed to develop or mature like everyone else. She'd often thought about how it would have felt if her parents had let her back home. Let her finish playing Final Fantasy Six. Let her... grow up. Surrounded by joy and love.

But it hadn't been possible.

And hearing that music play now made something pull deep inside of her. She had to go take a look at it. For the sake of closure, if nothing else.

She walked toward the teenage boy's room and knocked.

He grunted but didn't look up from the three large monitors on his desk. His room was a tech-lovers' dream. Each of his three monitors played something different. One was displaying the game he'd started up, another showed a live stream of a different game on Twitch, and another was open on some kind of chat thread that Kiera couldn't read from here.

"Hey," said Kiera. "I'm sorry if I frightened you before. I'm Kiera, the... cleaner."

The boy let out a mocking laugh. "A cleaner in a onesie?"

"Wearing a special outfit stops my clothes getting dirty," said Kiera. Nothing she said was an outright lie. She was just holding back on the truth, which was entirely appropriate, given the boy's age.

The boy turned back to his computer screens, but Kiera interrupted again. "What's your name?"

The boy paused a moment. "Didn't my dad tell you to expect me today?"

"No," Kiera replied. "He must have forgotten."

"Like he keeps forgetting to cut me a new front door key," said the boy. "Too busy drinking and sleeping around to remember his son "

Kiera swallowed away a pang of sadness. "Hey," she said, "you know, I'm pretty good at that game." She pointed to the monitor with Final Fantasy Six on it. "We could play together, if you like?"

The offer felt like it came from nowhere, but now that she'd made it, she couldn't take it back. She wanted to connect with the computer game she'd once played, yes, but it went deeper than that. She wanted to get to know Bastion's son, at least a little. She felt strangely responsible for him right now. She was the adult around here, after all, and the boy seemed detached and sad. Emotions she could relate to. It was almost like looking back at her own teenage self.

"I like my own space," said the boy defensively. "Aren't you meant to be working anyway?"

"Oh, I'm on a break," said Kiera. "That's why I changed into my own clothes, see?"

The boy scowled at her clothes, but when he noticed her punky style, with the ripped jeans, blue hair, and piercings, he softened and shrugged.

"Fine," he said. "If you insist."

Kiera didn't say anything, but took the spare seat beside him.

"I'm Tad, by the way."

"Hey Tad," Kiera said with a smile. "It's good to meet you."

She stayed silent now as the two of them communicated through the computer game. They weren't exactly comfortable like old friends around one another, but it felt like there was an understanding. A bond of trust.

Maybe Bastion's secret wasn't such a dark one, after all.

Chapter Ten

BASTION

B ASTION OPENED THE DOOR to his home with a lightness in his step.

He was excited to find out if Kiera had done what he had asked of her. It felt good to punish her for pushing herself too hard and also force her to take a much-needed break.

Part of him felt a thrill of anticipation; he wanted to see just how vulnerable Kiera had made herself for him. Had she sat still, just like he'd asked? Had she gone as far as wearing a diaper? It's not like he had a thing for diapers exactly. He just had a thing for a babygirl who could really let go. He knew how good Kiera would feel if she could let herself be regressed completely. He could just feel it in his bones that her Little was more little than she'd ever been before. A precious, sweet thing, needing more care and attention than she ever thought possible. The thought of being the one to provide that care excited him. The thought of *her* excited him.

As he opened the door, the thrill of anticipation instantly vanished. Kiera was not on the couch.

He felt a jolt of disappointment as he looked around, wondering if she was even in his house. Had she decided that his punishment was too hard? That this wasn't the lifestyle for her? No. Surely not. Not after the intimacy they'd shared on the phone just a few hours later.

Bastion tried to calm his racing heart. He had issues with abandonment, and he had to fight hard to stop them coming up again. Kiera was not going to abandon him. Besides, there was nothing to abandon. They hadn't even signed a contract yet. That was meant to be tonight's activity.

He was about to call out when he heard something unexpected: laughter. He looked upstairs toward the source of the sound and was surprised to see...

Oh, no.

Oh, shit.

His son's door was open.

It was Friday night. What a terrible father. Tad came home every other Friday afternoon after school for the weekend. In all the excitement about Kiera, he'd completely lost track.

He trudged upstairs with a heavy heart. Kiera had disappeared and he had neglected his fatherly duties. He was meant to be home early to let Tad in. He didn't have a spare key for the house, and honestly, Bastion had been delaying cutting him one.

Tad hadn't exactly been reliable lately. He was thirteen, so it's not like you'd expect a kid of his age to be reliable, but Tad was a hormonal teenager *and then some*. Tad was always a kinda reclusive child, and lately, he hadn't taken the break-up between his parents too well. He was cursing, stomping about, and slamming doors. Bastion felt like he barely knew him anymore. Tad wouldn't let him close.

"Hey, kid!" Bastion called out.

He heard more laughter. This time, it wasn't just Tad's. It was Kiera's too.

Well, this was interesting. It was very good to hear Tad laughing, he had to admit. It had been a long time. Maybe a year or more. But hearing him laugh with Kiera... that was strange. Tad never spoke to any of his friends, let alone had fun with them.

A horrible thought struck him as he neared the bedroom. Were they laughing at *him*? Laughing at the way he trudged so slowly up the stairs, or at his old man voice as he called out to them?

Quit putting yourself down, Bastion. You're not past it yet.

Bastion reached Tad's doorway and peeked inside the room. He could hear music now, and saw Tad and Kiera huddled around a computer screen, playing some kind of cartoonish game. It looked pixelated and old-fashioned, involving a fight between a goblin creature and some kind of... dragon-lobster hybrid? Man, he really *was* too old.

Tad and Kiera were so immersed in the game that they hadn't even noticed Bastion standing there. As he watched them, he felt a complex mix of emotions. He was relieved that Tad had made it home safe and sound, but also frustrated that he hadn't remembered to come home early for his son. He also felt guilty thinking about the punishment he had doled out for Kiera. He hoped that she hadn't been waiting on that couch for him naked or diapered when Tad had come back. Oh god.

Neither Tad nor Kiera looked traumatized, though. They were having a blast. In fact, as he looked at them playing together, they almost looked like they could be friends. They were probably closer in age to each other than Kiera was to him.

You're doing it again. Stop it. You're fine as you are.

Bastion cleared his throat. "Say, who wants Tex-Mex for dinner?"

As though he had uttered the magic words, both Kiera and Tad turned around.

Kiera smiled and clapped her hands together and even Tad looked almost happy. When Tad turned around to look back at the computer screen, Kiera gave Bastion a different look. A look of embarrassment, maybe? Or blame? He'd have to find out when they got a quiet moment later. For now, he had to order a serious apology takeout.

Bastion left Kiera and Tad to play and started heading back downstairs. On the way past Kiera's room, he paused. He had an urge to check the nursery, to make sure she hadn't packed her bags.

He unlocked the door, and the moment he opened it, he saw something lying on the floor. Something crinkly and white.

A diaper!

He went inside the room and looked at it, unable to hide his surprise.

Good girl!

She had done as he had asked. Next to the open diaper lay the plug that he had watched her insert earlier. She must have done as he'd asked, and then gotten changed after Tad came home. Poor girl. He hoped she hadn't had too big a shock. That sweetheart needed a reward tonight, not another punishment.

As he looked again at the diaper, he noticed a thin blue line down the front of it. My, my. She had *really* let herself go, huh? The thought of her sitting on his couch and wetting her diaper as she waited for him to come back was strangely arousing. She had done exactly as Daddy had asked. And now she was playing with Daddy's son like they were all in one big happy family.

He left the nursery, being sure to close and lock the door, and made his way downstairs. He opened up the details for his favorite Tex-Mex restaurant and ordered every single thing on the menu. Smoked brisket nachos. Queso flautas with salsa verde. *Torta ahogada*. Red tacos.

Chimichanga. Enchiladas. Capirotada. And about a million other things.

As he set the table ready for the food to arrive, he found himself humming happily. This was it. He had finally got the set-up he'd always wanted. His son. His babygirl. His Miami mansion. Nothing could possibly spoil this now.

*

Bastion picked up his pink glass tumbler full of virgin margarita. "Cheers, folks."

Tad and Kiera raised their tumblers too, and they all drank.

Bastion hoped that Kiera wasn't too nervous using a glass. He liked her to use a sippy cup so that she felt relaxed, but not when Tad was around. It was important that he kept his DDlg relationship completely private with Kiera, and she seemed to understand that. It wasn't appropriate for Tad to know about it. They would stipulate how it would all work in their contract: the times that they were able to engage in their lifestyle, and how they would protect Tad from it.

He wanted Kiera and Tad to feel at home and comfortable together, until he broke the news that Kiera was living here now. He knew it was a big revelation, but Tad had always said that his dad was useless at living alone. That the house was a dump and he was falling apart without a woman in his life. Now that Bastion could see that he was getting on so well with Kiera, he was excited to break the news to him.

"It's so good to sit down together like this," Bastion said.

"Do you normally eat dinner with your cleaner?" asked Tad, giving him a strange look.

Kiera blushed.

"Kiera is—" Bastion began, but Kiera interrupted.

"This food is so good," said Kiera, hungrily helping herself to more *flautas*.

That was weird. Had she interrupted him on purpose? Did she not want him to reveal her identity right now?

A thought crossed his mind. He hadn't spoken to Kiera about Tad yet. He hadn't held it back on purpose; they just hadn't had the chance to get to know each other so well yet. He should have probably mentioned it before asking her to move in with him, but he had been so distracted by the whole... situation in his pants... that he had hardly had a minute to think things through.

Damn. Had he screwed everything up? Was Kiera having second thoughts now that she knew about Tad?

Being sober was difficult. You actually had to deal with shit, and try to untangle the fucking mess you'd created for yourself while drunk.

"The tacos are making my lips burn," said Tad, reaching for his margarita.

"I dare you to put extra hot sauce on," said Kiera wiggling her eyebrows.

Tad looked at her. "Challenge accepted."

Before Bastion could utter a word of warning, the two of them were piling hot sauce all over their food, and then grabbing their throats and gasping for air as the chili attacked their mouths. It felt amazing to see them joking around, though. And it reassured him that everything was good with Kiera. Which meant that it was important to tell the truth.

When the hot sauce competition was finally over, and Tad admitted defeat while Kiera panted happily, Bastion took a deep breath and said, "I have an announcement to make."

Tad looked up from his plate and met his father's gaze. "What is it?"

Bastion hesitated for a moment before he spoke. "Kiera is going to be living with us now."

Tad dropped his fork in surprise. "What the hell, Dad?" he asked. "She told me she was the cleaner!"

Kiera's face dropped. She bit her lip awkwardly, but Bastion reached out and squeezed her arm. "It's okay," he said to her softly. "We'll figure it out." He turned back to Tad and said gently, "Kiera is my... girlfriend."

Kiera looked at Bastion with wide eyes, then her expression softened and she nodded slightly.

"That's right," she said, casting an apologetic look at Tad. "I'm sorry I didn't say anything. But it's true that I *am* your dad's cleaner too."

Tad grimaced. "So you just started fucking your cleaner, Dad?"

Bastion hated hearing his son cussing like this, but now was hardly the time to tell him off for it. Emotions were way too high for that. And it's not like he could blame this son. Bastion had handled this whole thing very badly.

"It's not like that," said Bastion. "Kiera was a... friend first. I know her through work. She started cleaning for me and then things developed very—"

Tad's chair screeched as he pulled away from the table, standing up and banging his fist on it. "Fucking liars, both of you!" He paused a moment, taking a deep breath, and then said: "I'm going back to Mom's house."

"Oh no you don't!" Bastion yelled, losing his cool. "Come back here right now!"

But Tad had already grabbed his backpack and was heading for the front door.

Bastion stood up. "Let me at least walk with you, son."

"Fuck you. Both of you." The door slammed.

Bastion looked at Kiera and saw tears running down her cheeks. "I'm sorry," he told her. "I handled that badly."

"Do you think you should follow him?" she asked.

"No," Bastion replied. "He's not going too far. I'll text his mother. Make sure he gets back okay. Tad needs time to cool off. This is a lot for him to take in." He grabbed his phone and punched out a quick text to Pauline. He wasn't about to tell her any of the details as she'd only use them against him. But he needed to make sure that Tad had got back safely.

"I feel horrible," said Kiera, putting her head in her hands. "I feel like I lied to him. Like I tricked him. I didn't even know you had a—" Kiera burst into torrents of tears now, and Bastion put his arms around her, holding her tight.

"It's okay, babygirl," he told her. "It's all okay. Don't worry. None of this is your fault. I messed up. I've been so distracted lately. Giving up the drink. Getting together with you. I'm a fool. But I'll fix this." He stroked Kiera's hair, loving the feel of her in his arms, feeling like he could stay like that forever. She was so beautiful, so amazing. He had to make sure they didn't lose her.

"Maybe I should stay at the hotel tonight," she said. "Give you some space."

"You're not going anywhere," he told her. "The three of us are going to work this out, okay?"

Kiera nodded, wiping her eyes with the palm of her hand. "I'm sorry," she whimpered. "It's just been a bit of a funny day. Kind of... up and down, you know? Things were going so well, and then..."

She burst into tears again, and Bastion was overcome with deep feelings of protection for her. "You don't have to worry about a thing, sweetheart," he said. "I'm the one who made this mess. I should have spoken to Tad about you. And I should have spoken to you about Tad. I've just been so caught up in everything recently that I got carried away. But I know what I want. I want my son to be happy. And I want you, Kiera. My babygirl. My darling."

He stroked her hair, holding her head against his chest so that she could hear how hard his heart thumped for her. "Until things got messy tonight, I was having the best time. We can get back to that. If it's what you want."

Kiera looked up at him. "As long as you'll be open with me from now on. We have to tell each other everything. I'm too paranoid to be with someone who's hiding stuff from me."

Bastion kissed the top of her head. "I'm with you a hundred percent, sweetie. I want you to know everything about me. And I want us to share our lives together. And by the way, it's not being paranoid to want to know the truth."

Kiera sniffed. "Tad's the most important thing, though," she said. "We need to make sure he's okay with this."

"He will be," Bastion said with certainty. "Tad wants me to be happy. He's just having trouble processing things right now. He'll come round. But right now, he needs a bit of space. And *you* need—," he tilted her face up to his with his chin and kissed her softly on the lips, "—some TLC."

"I'm not sure I'm in the mood for anything sexy right now, Daddy."

"It's okay, sweetheart," he said. "Daddy's not talking about sex. Daddy's talking about taking you on vacation."

"Vacation?" asked Kiera, sitting up straight. "Where?"

Bastion smiled. "Ever heard of a place called Liberty?"

Chapter Eleven

KIERA

K IERA WAS IN AWE as the car drove through the gates of Liberty. She had never seen anything like it.

The rolling hills and grassy fields stretched out before her, dotted with the occasional farmhouse and clump of trees. The sky was a deep blue, with a few scattered clouds, glowing brightly from the egg-yolk-yellow sun.

But what really made her stop and stare was the town itself.

In the center of the fields and hills was an old-fashioned western mining town, with wooden buildings and walkways, cobblestones, and a large clock tower in the center. There were people everywhere, going about their business and enjoying the sights. The town contained some unexpected quirks, though. There was a railroad track running around the town, with a pink and blue steam train chugging along in it. The sparkly gold lettering on its side spelled out: 'Liberty Loco'. There were string lights draped all over the trees and some of the buildings had been painted in bright colors, with cute murals painted on the sides.

"What is this place?" Kiera asked, turning to look at Bastion in amazement.

Bastion, who had been very secretive about the place until now, smiled. "This is Liberty. It's an old ghost town that a man called Haze brought to life. He bought this land and he's been rebuilding it for the past few years. It's a special place for people in the DDlg lifestyle."

Kiera felt her heart flutter as she took in the sight of the bustling town. She had heard stories about places dedicated to the Daddy Dom little girl lifestyle — ranches and nightclubs and hillside villages — but she had never imagined it could look like this. It was a far cry from the dark, seedy places she had imagined.

"It's beautiful," she said, her voice full of wonder. "Are we really staying here a whole week?"

Bastion nodded. "We sure are. You need a break. I need a break. This is the perfect place for us to be ourselves together."

Kiera felt a rush of relief. So far, Bastion and Kiera had kept everything to themselves. What happened in Scotland, and what had happened since. Even Peach and Daisy didn't know yet. It would feel so freeing to be able to explore their relationship without having to hide it while they were here.

They got out of the car, which Bastion had driven himself. Normally, he told Kiera that he'd get a driver, but it was important that Liberty's location remained secret. Kiera had enjoyed having her Daddy drive her. She had been pleased to see what a safe driver he was, never going over the speed limit, and making sure that she got rest breaks whenever she needed them. They'd stopped at a motel last night too when Bastion was too tired to drive anymore. They'd eaten meatball sandwiches in bed while watching cartoons and then fallen straight to sleep. Something told Kiera they'd be eating more than meatballs in bed tonight, though...

Now, Bastion took Kiera's hand and led her into the town. Everywhere she looked, there were people walking around, laughing, chatting, and enjoying each other's company. Bastion pointed out the various buildings they passed: a bakery, a general store, and a saloon called 'The Den'. Kiera couldn't help but stare at the people, who were all wearing different kinds of outfits. Some were in frilly dresses, with collars and cuffs, others wore diapers and romper suits, and some just wore jeans and T-shirts. Nobody looked embarrassed, no matter how far out their outfits were. A few girls were even walking around with two or three Daddy Doms!

"This is amazing," she said, her eyes wide with astonishment. She was carrying Blinky, her new pink teddy-bear, and normally, she'd have felt embarrassed about doing something like that, but not here. Here, she fitted right in.

Bastion smiled. "I knew you'd like it."

Suddenly, a voice called out from nearby. "Bastion! You made it!"

Kiera turned to see a tall, handsome man striding towards them. He had dark hair and super straight white teeth, and, unusually, he was wearing a bright Hawaiian shirt.

Bastion grinned. "Haze! Good to see you again, man."

Haze clasped Bastion on the shoulder. "It's been too long, my friend. I'm so glad you could make it." He turned to Kiera and smiled. "And you must be Kiera. It's a pleasure to meet you, young lady."

Kiera instantly felt very Little. She nervously returned the smile, squeezing Blinky tight for comfort. "It's nice to meet you as well, sir."

Haze chuckled. "Please, call me Haze. Although I'm sure your Daddy prefers 'sir' when you're in a scene together."

Kiera blushed.

Haze gestured around the town. "So, what do you think of Liberty?"

Kiera looked around in amazement. "It's incredible. I can't believe you built something like this."

Haze smiled. "Come, let me show you around."

Bastion and Haze walked off, deep in conversation, and Kiera hurried after them, excited to see more of the town.

Chapter Twelve

BASTION

H OW DO YOU KNOW whether someone is your soulmate?

Bastion looked at his Little girl. She looked exactly the same shape as the hole that had been cut out of his life until now. Her scent was intoxicating and grounding all at once. Her taste was his favorite taste.

More than anything, though, he felt a deep sense of calm when he was with her. Like he didn't have to worry about anything anymore. He'd found a place to plant his roots.

That's how you know.

As they breathed together in the soothing water of the bath house, his hard cock in her warm palm, he felt connected to her so deeply it was like they had known each other for lifetimes. Being here, in this old building, added to that feeling. It seemed to him that he could feel the spirits of those who had gone before, their joys and sorrows, the laughter and cries they had shared in this very chamber. He thought of the many hands that had touched the walls, and the bodies that had lain in this room over the years.

"Kiera," said Bastion softly. "I'm going to claim you now."

Bastion wasn't much of a religious man, but as he looked deep into her dark eyes, he said a silent prayer, asking for guidance in this new journey they were about to embark on.

Kiera looked as though she might be doing the same.

"It's okay, sweetheart," he said. "I won't hurt you. And if you want me to stop, just say so."

Kiera nodded.

"We'll be signing a contract tomorrow," Bastion told her, "with Haze to witness it. Until then, we won't be pushing any boundaries or testing out our limits. I simply want to slide my cock deep inside you, to fill you with myself. To make you mine. You understand?"

"Yes, Daddy," said Kiera. "I want that, too."

"Is there anything I need to know about? Have you been tested? Do you have any protection?"

"Yes to both," Kiera said shyly. "I'm clean, and I take pills."

"Good," Bastion replied. "I'm clean too. And I prefer it without condoms."

Ever since Kiera had curled her slender fingers around his dick, he'd had to work hard not to get too excited. His cock had only recently learned how to get hard again and it felt like an excited puppy. But what he was about to do with Kiera — he wanted to go slow, for it to last a long time. Maybe even forever.

"Now. Squeeze a little harder, sweetheart."

Kiera began to stroke him, the palm of her hand moving along the shaft of his cock. It felt so good in the water, the warm wetness making every sensation heightened and almost otherwordly.

"Just like that," he murmured. "Perfect."

Kiera smiled, clearly happy to be praised.

"Okay," he said. "I'm going to slide my cock into your pussy now. Tell me if it hurts and I'll stop."

"Okay," said Kiera. "I'll be okay."

Bastion flushed with excitement as he guided his cock to her entrance. He lifted her ass up a little, then held his breath as he dropped her down over the tip of his dick and nudged himself against her tight opening.

"Is it hurting?" he asked.

"No," she said. "I just need a minute."

"Okay," he said softly, running his fingers gently over her slit. "Take your time."

Bastion watched as she focused on relaxing her muscles. She wiggled her hips and thighs, then her butt, as though she was stretching out her muscles.

"Well done," he said, encouraging her. "No need to rush, darling." He stroked her opening some more, grazing her clit with his fingertips, just enough to get her fully aroused.

Kiera looked up at him and something in her expression changed as her pussy muscles suddenly relaxed and he felt her slide down his thick pole. Her mouth fell open as she took him in. "Ohhh..." she murmured. "Oh, Daddy!"

Kiera met his eyes and they both smiled.

"You feel so good," she said.

"So do you," he said. "So fucking good, darling." His first fuck in over a year. He'd forgotten how good it felt. But that was partly because it had never felt like this. Her pussy felt more perfect than any pussy he'd ever been inside before, but there was more to it than that. He was fucking someone he deeply cared about right now. Completely sober. Completely aware. His brain and her brain, totally connected. It was magical.

Kiera whimpered as she pressed her chest against his, his cock all the way inside her. The feeling of her hips against his groin, her naked skin against his, made him feel so good, so alive.

"Do you like it, sweetheart?"

"Yes," she said. "So much."

"You feel so tight, so good," he murmured. "I love how you squeeze my cock inside you. Do you want me to fuck you, Kiera?"

"Yes, Daddy," she whispered. "Please."

"I'm going to move now, just a little. But if it hurts, tell me."

Kiera nodded, then took a deep breath.

Bastion began to rock his hips then, sliding his cock in and out of Kiera a little, trying to get the rhythm going. Everything felt slower in the water, but that was good. That was how he wanted it just now.

"It feels perfect, Daddy," she whispered into his ear.

He felt a swell of pride at those words. He hadn't spoken to Kiera about her sexual experience thus far, but something in him knew to treat her like the fragile young thing she was. And she seemed grateful for it.

"You can go harder now, Daddy," she said. "If you like."

"Are you sure, sweetheart?"

"Yes, Daddy. I'd like it hard. I think it would feel good."

Bastion looked into his girl's eyes and saw no doubt, only passion. So he began to thrust harder, resting Kiera's back against the edge of the large bath so he could get deeper inside her.

She gasped, her mouth open, her eyes roving his face.

"Are you okay, sweetheart?"

"Yes," she said. "Oh yes. Don't stop, Daddy."

He didn't stop. He fucked her some more, alternating between fast and slow, bringing them both to the edge a few times, but always bringing it back before either of them had the chance to come.

"I want us to stay in this moment," he told her. "I don't want this to end."

"It doesn't have to," said Kiera. "It can go on forever, Daddy."

"It will," he said. "As long as you want it to. Tell me you understand."

"I do, Daddy. I know you won't hurt me, and I won't hurt you."

"Good girl," he said, kissing her, enjoying the feeling of that cool piercing against his lips. "That's my good girl."

"Thank you for making me your good girl."

"Thank you for making me your Daddy."

Bastion kissed her again, for what felt like hours. She was his. His woman, his submissive, his Little. She was his everything and he would protect her with his life.

"Please, Daddy," she whispered. "Please, I want to come."

"Not yet, babygirl," he told her. "Not until Daddy says you can."

Kiera moaned in protest and pouted, but he ignored her, reaching between her legs and finding her clit with his finger, gently tugging on it and rubbing it. She writhed and whimpered and moaned on top of his dick, her body tight with the effort of holding out. She was struggling now, he could tell, but she was suffering for him and he couldn't love her more for it.

Not that he did love her yet, of course. Unless...

Bastion sped up his thrusts and pumped his cock in and out of her faster now, rubbing her clit as hard as she could take it. He felt himself getting even harder and bigger, then he wanted to come so bad. So. Bad.

"Please... I can't hold it in any longer."

"Then come, darling," he said. "Come for Daddy."

"Ohhh!" squealed Kiera as she came. She clung to his shoulders, her body shaking and her pussy pulsing and squeezing his cock. Bastion's own orgasm took him by surprise. It was so intense and so sudden that he almost fell forwards. But Kiera grabbed his shoulders, brought him down to her, and kissed him, swallowing his cries as he came inside her.

*

Hand in hand, they exited the bath house and stepped out into the night. They were surrounded by a blanket of stars, so bright that it seemed as though they were putting on a special show just for the two of them. Bastion looked up at the night sky and felt a surge of hope and wonder.

There was so much time left for happiness.

He smiled down at Kiera, and she squeezed his hand. "Thank you, Daddy," she said. "For this trip. But also, for caring about me."

Bastion pulled Kiera toward him and kissed her tenderly. Those lips, that piercing. He could never tire of this girl.

They began to walk along the path back to the cabin Haze had set up for them, lit by the stars above. As they walked, Bastion put his arm around Kiera. "The same goes for you, by the way, babygirl. I felt pretty washed-up before we got together. So... thank you for caring."

"I care deeply," Kiera replied quietly.

When they reached the cabin, they stepped inside and lit candles, their shadows dancing in the flickering light.

Should he say it?

Just how deeply he cared?

No. He had to take things slow so he didn't scare her off. He was going to get everything right from now on.

They lay on the comfortable double bed in the back room of the cabin and undressed each other in silence. Bastion kissed Kiera's forehead, her cheeks, her lips, and said, "Never forget, Little girl, that I am here for you. You can dream as big as you dare, and together we'll make all your dreams come true."

Kiera smiled. "It's already happening, Daddy."

*

Bastion woke to the sound of an insistent knock.

He groaned. Kiera was still dozing in his arms and he didn't want to get up, but he knew he had to. They were expecting Haze to call on them with a copy of a DDlg contract. Haze was a pro at this stuff. He'd sorted contracts for most of the residents of Liberty, and Bastion knew that he'd do a good job for them.

Even though Bastion was excited about getting the contract signed, he didn't like the idea of leaving the warm bed. At the moment, he and Kiera were both naked and she was his little spoon. During the night, he had fucked her twice more, and she had kissed his cock and he had eaten her pussy so many times that their bellies were full of each other.

He'd been right too, about how good her piercing would feel when his dick was in her mouth. Cold and hard, pushing into the base of his shaft and the top of his balls. Pauline had never enjoyed giving him oral, but Kiera seemed over the moon when he instructed her to open wide for him. She'd even told him, before they fell asleep, that she wanted to go to sleep like that, with his cock parked deep in her mouth, resting on her warm tongue. But Bastion said there was no way he'd sleep like that. It was going to be difficult enough to sleep with her soft, sexy body in bed with him as it was.

Anyway, that was the night, and this was the morning.

He got out of bed quietly, letting Kiera sleep off all that sex for as long as possible. Once he was dressed and decent, and his morning wood had subsided, he opened the door.

"Bastion," said Haze. "You didn't forget, did you?"

Haze held up a freshly-printed contract, as well as a tray containing three takeaway coffees and a brown paper bag.

"Of course I didn't," said Bastion, ushering his friend inside. "We just had a... busy night."

Haze tutted. "Nothing too out there before the contract is signed, I hope."

Bastion ran his fingers through his hair. "Nothing too out there. But believe me when I say we're ready for this."

"Good," said Haze. Then, lowering his voice, he said: "You know, I like the girl. Make sure you take care of her. She's got the same look in her eyes that Winter had when she first came to me."

Bastion nodded, aware of the responsibility he was taking on. Kiera needed to be able to rely on him one hundred percent. Anything less would be a failure. No slip-ups with alcohol or not being honest with her. No creating chaos and drama in her life. She'd had enough of that already.

"I understand," said Bastion.

"I know you do," Haze said, slapping him on the shoulder. "Now, go get your girl. We have work to do."

Bastion went to wake Kiera, but she was already awake and mostly dressed, a look of excitement in her eyes. "Is that Haze out there?" she asked. "I can't believe we're signing our contract today!"

Bastion grinned. "You were sleeping like a baby a minute ago."

Kiera jumped up and down. "I couldn't sleep once I heard the door. It feels like Christmas Day!"

For a moment, Bastion was distracted by the thought of spending Christmas with Kiera. He imagined all the wonderful presents he would buy for her, and how happy she'd be as she opened them. How happy he'd feel unwrapping *her* on Christmas Day.

They went through to the main part of the cabin, and Haze had laid out three copies of the contract on the table, along with the coffees, and some delicious-looking croissants.

"Fresh from Dax's bakery," said Haze. "He makes the best croissants I ever tasted. He's Brie's Daddy, from the General Store, although she has two more Daddies: Silas and Zayn."

"How does that even work?" asked Kiera, sitting down and stuffing the end of the croissant straight into her mouth. "Mmmmmm."

"Probably a bit like that," replied Bastion, pointing at the croissant between her lips. "One in the mouth, one in the—"

"Daddy!" said Kiera, quickly swallowing her food. "That's very rude." She turned to Haze, her cheeks beetroot red. "The croissant is delicious."

"It's chocolate and almond flavor," said Haze. "Bastion, I gave you a plain one. Figured that was more you."

Bastion laughed. "Yup. I'm plain alright." He joined them at the table and took a gulp of strong, black coffee. Damn, that was good. Everything in Liberty seemed to taste that bit better than anywhere else.

"So," said Haze. "Everybody ready?"

Bastion looked at Kiera, reaching out for her hand. He gripped it tight, and she squeezed it back. "We're ready," he said.

Haze talked them through some of the basics of the contract, including the names that Kiera should call him ('Daddy' or 'sir') and the way that their DDlg relationship would run with Tad around. That was a little tricky, but they decided that when at home, they would keep all of Kiera's Little stuff locked away in the nursery, and they would confine their DDlg play either to the nursery, to Bastion's bedroom, or, if they were completely sure that Tad wasn't around, the kitchen.

"That's important to us," said Bastion. "Kiera enjoys being regressed at mealtimes."

Kiera blushed, but Haze made sure she felt completely at ease. "That's very normal," he said. "Food, naps, and baths are three of the simplest and most enjoyable times for Littles to get into Little Space."

"We'll have plenty of other opportunities to practice our relationship, though," Bastion told her. "Obviously all the schemes that my company runs are created for Daddies and Littles, and there are places like this where we can run away for the weekend and roleplay the entire time."

Kiera smiled. "It's exciting."

"Now, let's agree on a safeword. It's normally something that—"

"We already have one," cut in Bastion. "It's 'thistle'."

Haze looked at Bastion with a pleased nod. "Glad to see you've done some of this by the book already."

Kiera nodded. "Oh yes, Bastion has been a very good Daddy."

Bastion appreciated that comment, even though it wasn't wholly accurate. He could do better. He would do better.

"Let's go through your hard and soft limits, then," said Haze. "Are you comfortable doing this with me present?"

Bastion looked at Kiera. "There's no wrong answer, darling. How do you feel?"

"I don't mind as long as you're here, Daddy," she said.

"Alright," said Haze. "Then let's talk through *your* limits first, Kiera. Just look through the list and check the boxes in either the 'yes', 'no', 'maybe' column, depending on whether you feel it's something you're into."

"Don't be afraid to tell the whole truth," Bastion told her. "I know we've done some naughty stuff already, but it's important we get everything sorted properly now."

Kiera nodded. "Okay."

Bastion watched his sweet girl check the 'yes' box next to almost everything. Bondage. Blindfolds. Anal. His cock twitched in anticipation as he imagined doing each of those things with her. He couldn't wait to get some alone time with her again.

"I'm not sure about this one," said Kiera, pausing.

"Let's see," said Haze. "Ah yes. Predicament bondage."

"Do you know what it is?" Bastion asked.

Kiera shook her head, clearly a little embarrassed.

"It's a type of bondage where the submissive is placed in a position where they have to make a difficult choice," Bastion explained. "Often whichever choice you make results in some kind of physical or psychological discomfort."

"An example would be where the submissive is tied with their arms above their head," said Haze, "and given the choice between standing on their toes, causing leg fatigue, or letting their heels touch the ground, which causes their arms to ache from being stretched out. Or there's breath play, which Winter and I enjoy. But it's not for everyone."

"I don't think I like the sound of that," said Kiera.

"That's fine, babygirl," Bastion told her, stroking her back. "Just check the 'no' box and I'll make sure we never do it."

"I guess I'm not into anything that's too psychological," Kiera said. "Like, anything where I have to completely trust you. So... sensory deprivation. Anything involving blades."

"That's all totally understandable," Bsation told her. "I'll work hard to earn your trust because it's important for our relationship, but we'll never test it with any of the situations you don't like the sound of."

Kiera's shoulders seemed to relax slightly, and she checked the 'yes' box on everything else.

"Your turn now," said Haze.

Bastion hadn't expected to check the 'no' box for anything, but now that he thought about it, he realized that he had certain triggers.

"I don't want to do anything that triggers abandonment," he said. "So, if we're roleplaying, I don't think I'd enjoy roleplaying you acting up and walking out on me, or hanging up the phone on me. Nothing humiliating. Definitely no nasty comments about my cock. And," he sighed, "this is a hard one, but I don't want to do anything involving alcohol. I'm not going to drink, but... I'd prefer it if you didn't drink too."

He felt bad asking that of Kiera, but the fact that he'd managed to stay off alcohol since they'd gotten together was a big deal for him. If he saw her drinking or tasted booze on her, it might be hard for him to hold back. Plus, he didn't like the sound of a drunk Little. It sounded... risky.

"I don't mind, Daddy," Kiera said, looking him in the eyes. "I'm not much of a drinker, and when I do drink, well..."

He remembered what had happened between them in Scotland. It had been an exciting night, but one that he wished had played out differently. If they'd both been sober and done things right, then he wouldn't have left her afterward. What a jerk move.

"Right," said Haze when they were done talking through their limits, "it looks like we're almost there. All that's left to do now is to sign on the dotted line."

Bastion and Kiera both signed their names, and Haze signed as a witness, then left them alone together.

Ever since he had watched Kiera sign her name on that form, Bastion had felt an elation rising in him so powerfully that he had to take a breath.

"Are you okay, Daddy?"

Bastion nodded, pulling Kiera close to him and kissing her on the lips.

"I'm just very, very happy, darling," he told her. And it was true. He felt happier having signed this than when he signed his marriage contract. And even his divorce contract, too.

"Me too," said Kiera. "So... what now?"

Bastion looked at her. He wanted to do all the things on the contract with her, and then some. But they had some trust to build up with one another first.

"Babygirl," he said, "how would you feel about a playdate?"

Kiera's eyes sparkled.

Chapter Thirteen

KIERA

K IERA ARRIVED AT LIBERTY's Clocktower Play Area and was immediately overwhelmed. There were half a dozen Littles playing here, but she didn't know any of them.

I miss Peach and Daisy, she thought. People often mistook Kiera's aloofness for confidence, but the truth was, she was terrible at meeting new people. And old people. And... everyone.

"Sweetie?" Bastion asked. "Are you okay?"

"I'm fine," she said.

Bastion looked down at her. "Darling," he said gently but firmly, "it's important that you tell me the truth. I'm your Daddy and I can tell that something's troubling you."

"I'm... not good at meeting new people," Kiera said. "I guess that's to do with my trust issues."

"That's understandable," Bastion said, stroking her hand. "Trust is something that is earned over time, so it's okay to take small steps when building trust with someone. You don't need to trust anyone with any intimate details about yourself. But you could start by saying hello, or making small talk with the other Littles, or asking if you can join in with their game. Then, if you like, you can gradually build up to more vulnerable topics."

Kiera nodded. Having her Daddy guide her through this new situation felt so reassuring. She would probably never *fully* trust him, but she trusted him about as much as she trusted anyone.

Bastion bent down and put a gentle hand on her shoulder. "Ready for this, Kiera? Let's get you started."

Kiera nodded, looking around. She saw three Littles playing in the sandbox: a curvy woman with bouncy brown curls, who she recognized from yesterday. Haze had pointed her out as the owner of the General Store, while she had been out with her three Daddies. There was also a girl with pink hair and piercings, who looked even punkier than Kiera, as well as a girl with long dark hair and a white face, and gothic clothes.

"That must be Winter, Haze's Little," she whispered.

She watched the Littles as they played with brightly-colored plastic buckets and sand. They looked like they were having fun.

Kiera glanced at Bastion, unsure what to do. He smiled and nodded encouragingly.

"Why don't you go say hello? And if you're feeling comfortable enough, you could introduce yourself?"

Kiera took a deep breath, squeezing her Daddy's hand one last time, then she walked over to the sandbox and the two Littles. The curvy girl was giggling, and the pink-haired girl was making shapes in the sand with a stick.

"Hi," Kiera said, her voice wavering a bit. "I'm K-Kiera."

The girl stopped playing with the stick and looked up, her blue eyes wide with surprise.

"Hi, Kiera!" She said, her voice cheerful and friendly. "I'm Billie and this is Brie." She motioned over to the goth girl, who was currently burying her feet in the sand. "And that's Winter. Haze has told us all about you. Wow, I love your blue hair!"

The other two Littles waved. "Hey, Winter!"

Kiera felt suddenly much more at ease. She smiled back and knelt next to them in the sand. "What are you guys doing?"

"We're making a mega-castle!" Winter said, already scooping sand with her bucket. "Here, do you want to join us?"

Kiera quickly joined in and was amazed by how comfortable she felt when she had something to occupy her. It turned out that they were trying to make the biggest sandcastle in the entire world. Billie kept drawing the plans in the sand while Brie did most of the work, and Winter was too busy burying her body parts to be of much help. They seemed very glad to have Kiera on board, as she had gotten very good at making sandcastles on Miami Beach, and turned out to be a valuable member of the team.

Soon the three of them were playing happily together.

"So, what's Miami like?" Winter asked. "Is it worth a visit?"

"Depends what you're into," said Kiera.

"She's into goth stuff," said Brie mischievously. "Like, coffins and spiders."

"I like other stuff too!" Winter insisted. "Sometimes." She stuck out her tongue at Brie, and the two of them fell about laughing.

"It's good if you like blue skies and palm trees," Kiera said. "And water. Lots of water."

"It sounds amazing," said Brie. "I'll probably go with the triplets when they're a little older."

"Triplets?" Kiera asked.

"She has three babies!" said Billie. "They're adorable."

Kiera thought that seemed strange. Being a Little and having babies. She wanted to ask how it worked, having three Daddies and three babies, but decided it was best not to pry. She obviously had a lot to learn about the lifestyle, though. Everyone had their own way of navigating it.

They continued to chat as they worked, and soon, their sandcastle castle was so big that the three of them could sit inside it.

As Kiera looked up at the sky, a tune started playing above them. Kiera recognized it as the tune to 'Pop Goes the Weasel.' Halfway through the tune, bubbles started shooting out of the clock tower.

"That's so cool!" Kiera said. "I can't believe it does that every hour."

"Time for a juice break, Kiera!" Bastion called. "Honey, why don't you come over here and I'll pour you a juice and give you a little snack."

Bastion had been sitting quietly nearby this whole time, making Kiera feel reassured by his presence. She was happy to have him here, but she felt a little conflicted, as she didn't want to leave her new friends.

"Come on, sweetie," said Bastion. "It's important you stay hydrated."

"You better go," Billie whispered. "Daddies don't like it when you keep them waiting."

Kiera got up and brushed off her clothes. As she walked toward Bastion, she felt a thrill of joy run through her. This felt pure, and it gave her hope that maybe every day could be like this from now on. Maybe people *were* good, after all.

She sat beside Bastion and he gave her a carton of juice.

"Don't drink it all at once," he told her. "I have a healthy snack for you as well." He opened up a bag of trail mix. "Make sure you chew the big pieces properly. Don't want you choking."

Kiera giggled. "I know how to eat trail mix, Daddy. I'm not an *actual* kid."

Bastion looked down at her lap. "Do you need a diaper?" he asked her. "It's common for Littles to get so lost in their play that they wet themselves from time to time."

Kiera giggled again. "I'll be okay," she said. "I'm not sure I'm ready to wear diapers in public yet."

Bastion nodded. "No problem. They're just here if you need them, honey."

Kiera looked up at him. "Bastion, why do you like to regress me so much? You know, right back to being a baby?"

He looked at her, pausing a moment before answering. "I guess I think it's important to try going back as far as you can, then you know what you like best." He ran his hand through his hair. "It feels natural to me that being regressed back to being very small would feel very good. When I was very small, I felt truly happy," he said, his voice gentle.

"It's hard to think of you as being very small," Kiera said, casting a glance at Bastion's broad shoulders and tight abs. Even thinking about his impressive body made her start to ache with lust.

"My happiest time was when I was around two or three," said Bastion. "I used to pretend I was a superhero at home with my mom. We would fly around the living room together like there was nothing in the world that could get in our way. It was a time of innocence and warmth, and I want you to be able to experience something similar."

"Sounds awesome," Kiera said, thinking back to her own childhood and feeling similarly fond memories of being so small. Except that she didn't remember her mom and dad being quite as generous with their time as Bastion's. Most of her games were played alone.

Bastion's fists clenched. "That was before my cheating dad walked out on us and my mom started drinking heavily. Then it all fell apart."

Kiera's eyes widened. She had no idea. "Do you think that's why you have abandonment issues?"

Bastion shrugged. "Partly that," he said. "Partly the way my ex, Pauline, left me. She cheated on me, then left me for a younger man."

Poor Bastion. He probably had trust issues too. And Kiera could see why he seemed worried about feeling old now. "I see. Thank you for telling me, Daddy. I know it's not easy."

"With you, Kiera, it *is* easy," Bastion said, giving her a playful prod.

"Hey!" she said, giggling. Then, she looked up at Bastion with serious eyes. "I guess I thought you wanted to regress me so small as a kind of control thing. But I get it now. You want me to be truly happy."

"Exactly," Bastion replied.

"So... I'll be as Little as you want me to be."

"Only as long as you're enjoying yourself."

"I will be," said Kiera. "I am."

She looked around Liberty, taking in a deep breath of fresh Texan air. This town was inspirational. Built from tatters. It was time for her to build herself in just the same way. One step at a time. As far as she could go. And with her Daddy here to guide her, she knew that she could go all the way.

*

The week in Liberty had flown by. They'd gotten to know the residents really well, and they'd had plenty of alone time too.

Bastion had set up a nice routine for them. He would fetch coffee and pastries from the bakery every morning and bring them back to Kiera at eight o'clock, then Kiera would have a playdate for a couple of hours until lunch. Back at the cabin, Kiera wasn't allowed to say a word to Bastion until she'd made him come using her mouth, then they'd talk about all the fun stuff she'd done that morning. In the afternoon, they'd take a walk, and Bastion would choose a secluded spot for a sexy picnic, then in the evening, Bastion would cook for Kiera, then she'd wash the dirty dishes in the nude while he watched. After that, he'd tie her up and fuck her for as many hours as he could manage, then he'd give her a bubble bath and read her a bedtime story.

Of course, he'd spanked her a lot too. She liked to be good for her Daddy, but he invented all sorts of excuses to do it, and she didn't mind. Her butt ached and stung from all the attention his palm had given it, but every single time, it made her pussy so wet that she'd begged him to fuck her straight afterward.

The old Kiera might have been embarrassed about these relationship dynamics, but not anymore. Kiera had learned a lot in Liberty, about how different relationships worked, and about how it was possible to make the lifestyle work in all kinds of ways, including if you had kids. She'd learned about the soft and hard limits that would dictate the sexier parts of her new relationship. And she'd seen how kind and encouraging Bastion was, and she'd learned how good he felt inside of her.

Most of all, she'd really started to trust him. Maybe not fully. Maybe that would never happen. But coming as far as she had done felt like real progress.

But Liberty wasn't where Kiera belonged. She needed to be here now. She needed to learn the rhythms of her new life with her Daddy. She needed to grow her business. Plus, she was eager to catch up with her friends, to tell them everything that had been going on with her. Finally, she knew that she was ready to talk to them about Bastion, and she couldn't wait.

So, it was good to be home. Not just back in Miami, but in this big glass-filled mansion that was now her actual home.

"I think I'm on cloud nine, Daddy," she said, as Bastion pushed open their front door. "I keep having to pinch my arm to remind myself that it's real."

"As long as you don't hurt that precious arm of yours," he told her, "otherwise there'll be consequences, young lady."

Kiera shut the front door behind her. She felt a strong tingle in her panties. "What kind of consequences, Daddy?"

He turned around to face her, pushing her up against the wall, thrusting his tongue between her lips as his hand traveled down her stomach and between her legs. He cupped her pussy, and then pinched her on the bottom.

"Let's just say that the pain in your butt cheeks will remind you not to hurt any other part of your body for weeks."

Kiera shivered. "Sounds serious."

Bastion pressed his hard body against hers, and she felt the warmth of his already-erect cock nudging at her panties.

Do it, Daddy, she thought. *Take me right here, up against the wall.*

"Do you have any idea how much I wanted to fuck you the whole drive home?" he whispered in her ear, grinding his crotch against her, showing her how aroused he was with every tiny movement.

"I think I can guess," she whispered back.

He unbuttoned her jeans, then slid his hand inside her panties, dipping his finger into her already-wet pussy and then using her moisture to rub her clit.

"I'm gonna fuck you pretty much constantly whenever I'm not at work," he told her. "I hope your sweet little pussy's ready for it."

"It's ready," she gasped.

He yanked down her panties and then kneeled in front of her.

"It's not ready until I say it is, young lady," he said, running his tongue up and down her slit.

She grabbed fistfuls of his hair to steady herself as he pleasured her with his tongue. As he flicked the tip of his tongue back and forth over her clit, he used his fingers to stretch open her pussy.

"Oh, D-Daddy, you're gonna m-make me…"

This was all so sudden, so unexpected, that she was driven straight over the edge of a cliff she never even saw coming. Her eyes rolled back, her pussy clenched around his fingers, seeped wetness all over his tongue, and he drank her up greedily.

"Mmmm," he said at last, looking up at her. "Better than alcohol."

"So… I guess I'm ready now?" Kiera asked, her speech slurring slightly from the intense climax she'd just experienced. "To get fucked all night?"

Bastion tutted. "Naughty girl. Only Daddy's allowed to use the 'f' word. You'll get a punishment if there's any more naughtiness."

Kiera bit her lip, trying not to encourage him to punish her. She wanted to make sure that she got the prize of her Daddy's cock, thrusting in and out of her all night long.

"In answer to your question," said Bastion, pulling up her panties and jeans and then standing up again, "you're almost ready, yes. But I have to put something in your tummy first." He laid his palm flat against her stomach.

"Um… a baby?" she guessed, confused.

"No, silly," he said, bopping her nose. "Bagels. You stay here and relax, and I'll go grab some for us. I've been hearing your tummy rumbling ever since we left West Palm Beach."

"Oops," said Kiera, smiling. "I didn't realize I was hungry until I got back in the car."

"It's okay, babygirl," said Bastion. "I like doing things for you." He flexed his bicep. "Hunter-gatherer, see?"

Kiera laughed, looking down at his crotch. "You'd better readjust your underpants before you get the bagels, Daddy. Otherwise they might just throw the bagels onto your pole like a game of ring toss."

Bastion looked down at the tent in his pants and readjusted himself. "I'll remember that mischievousness," he said, waggling his finger at her. "Now, go relax on the couch for me. I won't be long."

Bastion left and Kiera walked into the large empty mansion, unable to believe that this really was hers now. Obviously, Bastion had asked her to move in with him before they'd gone to Liberty, but everything felt so much more real now. They'd signed on the dotted line.

The place looked spotless. Bastion had ordered not one but three cleaners to make all the living spaces sparkle for their return. He didn't want Kiera feeling like she had to lift a finger. There was a pile of belongings that had been brought over from Kiera's apartment as well. It felt like such a relief to never have to worry about going back to that hellhole ever again.

She plopped down onto the couch, realizing that she just wasn't very good at relaxing.

Maybe I could work on some ideas for my bubble bath company?

She took a notebook out of her backpack, which she always carried with her when she went traveling, and she began writing down some of the scents that reminded her of Liberty. Smoked brisket, bluebonnets, cedar, mesquite, and the rubber balls in the ball pit near the clocktower.

She was engrossed in her notes when she heard the key turn in the lock. She hoped her Daddy wouldn't be angry to see her working.

"It's not what you think, Daddy!" she called out. "The thing is, I find this kind of work very relaxin—"

Her words trailed off as she saw who was standing in the doorway.

It wasn't Bastion at all.

It was a woman.

Slender and blond. With impossibly large red lips and even more impossibly large breasts. And...

She was heavily pregnant.

"You must be Kiera," she said, running her hands over her large belly.

Kiera swallowed. "Yes," she squeaked. "And you are—"

"Pauline," said the woman. "Bastion's former lover. And the mother of his child." She glanced down at her round stomach. "Well. His *two* children."

Chapter Fourteen

BASTION

B ASTION'S ERECTION DIDN'T SUBSIDE the entire time he was
out. He ordered the bagels with an ache in his dick so strong
that he was tempted to run off before they were ready so he could be
with her.

His body was designed for her. His cock yearned for her. His heart
beat for her.

His whole life, he had wanted a love like this. Good and wholesome.
Not fueled by parties or narcotics or social pressure. Just a beautiful
partnership between two perfect soulmates. A man who wanted to
care for a woman, and a woman who appreciated his care.

He had to resist the urge to whistle or skip as he walked back to his
mansion. He felt ten years younger since the trip to Liberty. Over the
next few days, he expected to feel even younger still.

Who knew there was so much life in him yet? So much blood in his
veins? In his cock?

As he opened the front door, he felt his dick straining to get out of
his pants and into his lover's pussy.

*Not so fast, Mister. We have to let the girl eat first. She needs to build
up her stamina.*

But as soon as he was in the house, he heard a voice that made his dick go instantly limp.

It was her.

Pauline.

He could see her from behind, standing there in the drab pea coat she wore when she was pregnant with Tad. He hated that coat, and he never understood why it had been so expensive.

"My nose is like a bloodhound's right now," she was saying to Kiera. "I can smell everything. The cleaning products you've used are full of bleach and toxic chemicals, no doubt. I should leave before it does me any harm. In fact, I—"

"Pauline," said Bastion, cutting her off. "What the hell are you doing here?"

Pauline spun around to look at her, and that's when he saw it: a nine-month pregnant belly full of baby.

"I came to talk," Pauline said. "As soon as Tad told me the truth about you and your little... slave." She looked over her shoulder at Kiera.

Bastion glanced over at her, and his heart broke when he saw how sad she looked.

"We need to talk about the baby, Bastion," said Pauline, rubbing her belly. "About the custody arrangements, and the—" she paused, "—child support payments."

Bastion frowned. "What are you talking about, woman? And how did you even get in here? You gave me back your key."

She shrugged. "I took Tad's. That's how he 'lost it.'"

"You stole his key?"

"You were meant to cut him a new one straight away. How was I to know you'd keep forgetting to do that for your own son? Some father you are."

Some mother you are.

Just then, Kiera stood up. "I should... leave you to it."

"No," Bastion boomed, louder than he intended. "You stay there, sweetheart." He looked at his ex-wife. "Pauline, you're the one who needs to leave."

Pauline laughed. "This is the kind of man you're with, Kiera," she said. "Puts a baby in your belly then leaves you to fend for yourself."

"That's a lie," said Bastion, with gritted teeth. "You left *me*, and anyway, that baby's not mine. Must be lover boy's."

Pauline shot him a look. "Liar. You're the only man I've ever had sex with without protection. Of course it was you."

Bastion walked over to Kiera, reaching out for her hand, but she pulled away.

"Bastion?" she said in a small voice. "Tell me the truth. Is the baby yours?"

Bastion looked down at her, the poor scared thing. He couldn't believe that her faith in him was already being tested, and so soon after telling her she could trust him. He had to find a way to help her believe him.

"No," said Bastion.

At the exact same moment, Pauline said, "Yes."

Kiera looked between them like a rabbit caught in headlights. "I... I'm going upstairs," she said. "To pack my stuff."

"Is she going up to that perverted little nursery you made?" Pauline asked loudly. "The one you tried to fuck me in before I ran away? She should run away too, if she knows what's good for her."

Bastion was so angry he was practically exploding. That's not how any of this happened at all. He had shown Pauline the nursery, yes, hoping that opening up to her about his true self would help mend their broken relationship. But the moment he'd shown it to her, she'd slammed the door.

She'd stayed with him for a full year after that, but held his revelation against him. She said he was filthy and 'wrong' and used it as an excuse to cheat and do god only knows what behind his back, finally leaving him for a twenty-year-old 'sound healer 'from Williamsburg, New York. Seriously. A sound healer.

During the entire year before she left, she was drunk more than she was sober, out more than she was in. Bastion knew for a fact that the baby wasn't *his* because he didn't get hard once, let alone come anywhere near her. Not even close. Not even when she drunkenly tried to initiate something with him.

He just hoped Kiera believed him when he told her all this.

"You need to go," he told Pauline, "right now."

Pauline froze, tears coming into her eyes. "Help me, Bastion," she pleaded. "You know, Ezra left me. For an eighteen-year-old. I have no-one."

Immediately, Bastion thought of Tad. He'd been living with his mom at Ezra's hipster apartment in Wynwood for the past six months. And now he had to leave that and find someplace new all over again.

Poor kid. He had so much to deal with right now. No wonder he'd been so mad at Bastion for the past few months, thinking Bastion had abandoned Pauline after getting her pregnant. His heart bled when he thought about his own kid keeping those feelings bottled up. Why hadn't he mentioned Pauline's pregnancy even once? Because Bastion hadn't made any time for Tad, that's why. Well, things were going to change.

Bastion shook his head. "You have your parents. Go stay with them. And let Tad stay with me."

Pauline laughed. "Tad doesn't want to stay with you and your little *whore*. In fact, he hates you so much that he's waiting out there in the car right now. He doesn't even want to step foot in this place." She pointed outside at the street. Bastion looked out the window and saw Pauline's silver Porsche 911.

"Let me talk to him," said Bastion.

He was trying not to let it show, but right now, his pulse was racing. He felt in danger of losing his girlfriend and his son, all at once.

Just then, he heard a noise on the stairs and saw Kiera coming down with her bag.

"Sweetheart," he said, "let me explain. This isn't what you think. Don't leave me."

Kiera's stony expression said it all. "This is all too much for me, Bastion, whatever I think," she said. "I don't need all this drama. It's not healthy for me."

Bastion went over to her, but she backed away from him.

"Darling," he said quietly. "Please."

But Kiera shook her head, staying firm.

Bastion took a step back, respecting her need for space, but he couldn't give up. Kiera was one of the two best things to ever happen to him. He had to win her back, and then win back his son right after.

"Kier—" he began, but he was interrupted by a wet, sloshing sound.

"Shit," Pauline muttered, looking down.

Bastion followed her gaze and saw that his sparkling clean floor was now splattered with a pale, greenish liquid.

Oh... fuck.

Pauline's waters just broke. They weren't meant to be that color, were they?

"Take me to the hospital, Bastion," said Pauline. "Something's wrong."

Bastion looked at his ex-wife, a woman who'd had so much plastic surgery lately she was unrecognizable from the woman he first knew. A woman who had bullied him and cheated on him throughout their entire relationship. A woman who always took things too far, who always asked too much. And yet... she Tad's mom. And she needed help.

Bastion looked at Kiera. "I'm so sorry," he said to her, "but I have to do this."

Kiera's expression looked panicked and angry all at once.

Bastion's heart ached for her, but he had to take control. "Kiera, I'm going to need to ask you a huge favor," he said. "Can you look after Tad for me until I get back? Pauline. Look at me. I'm gonna get you to the hospital, okay? We'll take your car."

No way I'm getting that woman's amniotic fluid on the seats of my Bentley Continental GT, thank you very much. Even if this is an emergency.

Bastion looked at Kiera. "Sweetheart?" he asked softly. "Is that okay with you?"

Kiera's shoulders dropped. "Fine," she said quietly. "I'll do it."

Bastion snatched Pauline's car keys out of her hand and guided her to the door. It was time to take his ex-wife to the hospital, to help her give birth to a baby that was definitely not his.

Great. Just great.

*

The Miami streets glowed eerily in the streetlights at three a.m.

Bastion yawned, trying to focus on the roads. It had been a long night. He'd drunk three cups of strong coffee, and his veins fizzed with caffeine and adrenaline in spite of his sleepiness.

The bottom line was that Pauline and the baby were going to be alright. Apparently, Pauline had an infection of the placenta called *chorioamnionitis*, which gave her waters that greenish color. But the doctors at the private clinic had known exactly what to do, and within a couple hours, the baby had been delivered, and both mom and baby's condition had been stabilized. They were both on a course of antibiotics to resolve the problem.

In spite of himself, Bastion had waited to make sure everything was okay. How could he not? He wasn't a monster. Even after everything Pauline had put him through, they had a history together. They had a *son*. If something had happened to Tad's mom...

Damn. He couldn't even think about that.

He parked and went up to his front door, unable to believe that only a few hours ago, he'd been coming in here with Kiera, with a horny hard-on and a plan to stay up all night fucking his Little princess into oblivion.

He pushed open the door, wondering If Kiera would still be awake, would still be furious with him. He'd tried calling her from the hospital a couple times before it got too late, but she hadn't answered.

Inside, the house was silent. He took off his shoes and walked softly down the hall, hoping not to wake anyone. As he neared the door of the living room, he heard gentle snoring.

He peered inside and saw Kiera, curled up on the couch with her thumb in her mouth and all her bags at her feet.

Opposite her, on the other couch, was Tad. He was fast asleep, still clutching his video game controller. The game, up on the huge television screen on the wall, was showing a shot of two people in the middle of a fight, but they were frozen and silent.

Bastion sat down beside his son, pulling a blanket over him to make sure he was warm. Poor boy. Only felt like yesterday that *he* was being born.

Tears welled up in Bastion's eyes.

"Your mom's gonna be okay," he whispered.

He couldn't even begin to imagine what Tad had been through over the last six months. He felt terrible that Tad hadn't trusted him enough to talk to him about his mom being pregnant. Why not? Probably because he'd seemed so chaotic, so unstable, drinking too much, and living like a pig in a sty.

Well, not anymore. Bastion was going to be a dependable father, and a dependable Daddy to Kiera, too.

He stroked his son's soft brown hair, kissed the top of his head, and then walked over to Kiera. He looked around for a blanket to keep her warm too, but as he did so, Kiera woke up.

"Oh," she whispered. "You're back." She paused. "Is everybody alive?"

"Everybody's alive," Bastion whispered back. "Now listen, there's so much I want to talk to you about. Do you want to wait until morning, or—"

Kiera put her finger to her lips. "You'll wake Tad," she said. She grabbed her bags and stood up, then walked into the corridor.

Bastion followed her.

"I meant what I said," she told him, her voice still low. "This has all gotten too much for me. You said before you were going to tell me everything. But now, I don't know who to trust. And I don't know where I stand. I can't be with you, Bastion. And I can't be his—" she pointed at Tad, "—nanny, or whatever. I'm sorry. This is all too... I have to... Goodbye."

"No," Bastion said firmly, a little too loudly, but thankfully, Tad didn't stir.

Kiera looked up at him defiantly. "I'm not your submissive anymore, Bastion," she said, her voice quiet and wavering. "I'll see you around."

With that, she turned and left, closing the door quietly behind her. The click the door made as it shut was the saddest sound Bastion had ever heard in his whole life.

Fuck this, Bastion thought. *I need a whiskey.*

Chapter Fifteen

KIERA

KIERA TRUDGED THROUGH THE moonlit streets of Miami. The luxury mansions loomed over her like giants, their shadowy, ornate facades reminding her of the life she had walked out on. She didn't want to be out here, but what else could she do?

She thought back to the events of the evening, to her last conversation with Bastion. He had been so desperate, so hurt. She had wanted to stay, wanted to explain herself fully, but the words had escaped her. She had been the one to walk away, so why was she left with this tremendous sense of loss?

She shook her head, pushing away the bad thoughts as she kept walking. She had no idea where she was going, but her feet seemed to have a destination all of their own. She shuffled, aimless and alone, until she reached the beach.

There, she sat on the sand, took Blinky out of her bag, kicked off her shoes, and exhaled.

The sand felt soothing beneath her toes, and the sound of the waves crashing against the shore filled her with a strange sense of comfort. She watched the world around her in the dark, her thoughts turning to everything that had led her here. Following Daisy to Miami. Getting mad at Peach for her shotgun wedding to Isaac. Uprooting her business and almost running it to the ground in the process.

Business had never been booming, but at least she'd had a few connections back in Connecticut. A couple of buyers at local stores who had ordered the occasional bottle of bubble bath. Here, though, she had nothing.

There had been a strange sense of relief in her the moment she had walked away from Bastion. If she put some distance between them, built some barriers, then he couldn't hurt her anymore...

But now, she was suddenly filled with a deep sense of regret. What had she done? Why had she walked away? She had been so afraid of the complicated reality of life with Bastion. A son. An ex-wife. A new baby that may or may not have been his, depending on what and who she believed. There were so many hoops to jump through to find happiness. So many leaps of faith to make. The whole thing made her feel so panicked, so unsure, so vulnerable. So, she had chosen to leave for the sake of simplicity. For the sake of keeping herself on an even keel.

But now that she was alone, she felt more panicked than ever. She had no idea what the future held.

Kiera looked up at the night sky, filled with stars, and sighed. It was almost as if the stars were speaking to her, reminding her of all the mistakes she'd made in her life. Each sparkling pinprick a fiery regret.

You're always running, Kiera. You never stand still.

She stayed on the beach cuddling Blinky until the sun began to rise, watching the horizon and the waves, trying to convince herself that this was what she needed. To be alone, away from the world and its drama.

As the sky slowly changed from black to purple, Kiera slowly rose and began walking across the sand. As she walked, she thought of

Daisy and Peach, the people who understood her. She had no idea what would happen next, but at least she had her friends. They were enough.

She pulled her phone out of her pocket and took a moment to think. Daisy was still on her neverending whopper of a honeymoon. But Peach would be around. Pregnant, loved-up Peach, whose life seemed to be a permanent honeymoon, even though she wasn't going anywhere. She pressed Peach's call button and waited.

"Hello?" said Peach through a yawn.

"Hey," said Kiera. "I'm sorry to wake you."

"What time is it?" asked Peach. "Oh. I see the clock. Six o'clock! Yikes. I need to get up in a minute."

"You do?"

"Yeah, I'm at the ranch. Got to check and count the cattle and feed the horses."

"Oh," said Kiera, crestfallen. "You're at the ranch."

"Yeah," said Peach. "I'm sorry. I'm going to be away quite a bit for a while, now we've got some livestock. Eventually, we plan to come back to Miami every weekend, but while we're setting up here, there's so much to do…"

Peach's ranch was in Okeechobee. She and Isaac had been setting up since right after they got together, but Kiera hadn't been out to visit it yet. Peach said the place was still a mess and she wanted to make it hospitable at the very least.

"Did you need something?" Peach asked, sounding much more awake now.

"Yeah… no," said Kiera. "Just hoping for a catch-up."

And a place to live. But I can't ask you that. I won't let myself.

A few years ago, Kiera had been homeless. She'd lived on the streets, fending for herself. It was a while ago, but something like that never leaves you. The feeling that you're on your own in the world. That you can't even trust your own sleeping bag to keep you warm.

Back when Kiera was fifteen, a newbie to the homeless life, she'd started out trying to make friends with other displaced people. She'd found herself a group of slightly older teens quite easily. They let her sleep near them and shared the odd bit of food with her. But then, one day, while she was out begging for money, they'd stolen all her stuff. Her tent. Her food. Her sleeping bag. And the one thing she loved more than anything else: her childhood stuffie, a dog called Max.

After that day, Kiera had vowed to never trust anyone ever again. And if she ever managed to stop being homeless, she swore she'd never accept charity, no matter how much she needed it.

"Aw, you sound down, Kiera," said Peach. "Why don't you head over to the ranch for a few days? It's still kind of a mess here, but there's a spare room, and a warm fire, and my Daddy Isaac has been making enough stew to see us through about ten apocalypses." She giggled.

"Oh man, that sounds great," said Kiera, genuinely meaning it. "But... I'm pretty busy right now. I'm heading out of town for a while myself, actually. Got a few business leads to follow up on at luxury spas around Florida. Thought I'd make it into a vacation." That bit wasn't true. None of it was. But she hated it when her friends felt sorry for her. It didn't feel like an equal friendship if she was the object of their pity all the time. Especially now they were married and living their perfect lives. Kiera had to invent a little perfection of her own. "Maybe next time."

Maybe next time when I can afford even the bus ride out to you.

"Okay," Peach said. "No worries. Sounds like fun! You only just had a vacation too, you lucky sausage."

"Yeah. Guess I got the bug now." Kiera hadn't told Peach that she'd gone to Liberty. She'd just said that she was getting out of town for a few days, and Peach had been so busy with the ranch that she hadn't even questioned it. Showed how much they'd grown apart.

"Well, I'd better go," said Peach. "Daddy Isaac's whispering naughty things in my ear and if I don't go out to help him with the animals he's going to do naughty things to my bottom that I can't even say out loud."

Kiera said a quick goodbye to her friend.

Naughty things to her bottom.

Bastion should have been doing naughty things to *her* bottom right now. She thought about the feeling of that blue butt plug he'd made her wear, how wide open it had stretched her back passage, ready for his nice big cock to slide in. She thought about their night of passion in Liberty, and how good it had felt when he'd gone down on her in the entrance to their — *his* — mansion last night.

The whole situation sucked. Bastion was the Daddy of her dreams. It's just... her dreams weren't half as complicated as real life. So it was time to put up barriers again, to make sure she stayed protected.

Look after number one.

Not knowing what else to do, Kiera walked in the direction of her old apartment. The one her landlord had been about to throw her out of for being late with her rent payment.

Maybe there was a way she could talk him around? It was unlikely he'd have found someone else to stay there already. And if she really worked hard on her business, she could probably pay her rent in a week or two. She could spend the day visiting bath and body shops. There must be tons of places in Miami that would like her products.

Kiera heaved her bag along, feeling the weight of those products in her bag. They were one of her only worldly possessions. She took them everywhere with her, feeling more and more weighed down by them by the day.

Well, not anymore. Kiera was going to sort herself out now. She wasn't going to rely on anyone else to save her. She was the heroine of her own story.

*

Kiera arrived at her old apartment building and felt a wave of sadness wash over her. It was such an ugly, dilapidated building, so different from the beautiful mansion she'd just left. She stuffed Blinky into her bag, then trudged upstairs and knocked on the door opposite her old place.

The smell of stale cigarettes and cheap booze filled the air when the landlord opened it. He was a slimy, sleazy man with a nasty smirk on his face as he looked her up and down.

Kiera tried to stay strong, trying to keep her composure. She couldn't run away, especially when this was her only option.

"Hi," she said. "I was hoping we could chat about me taking back my old apartment?"

The landlord frowned. "You know what time it is, kid? You better have got me out of my warm bed for a good reason. You got the cash?"

Kiera took a deep breath. "Um, no. Not yet. But I promise I'll have it in a week or two." She clenched her jaw. "And I'll pay you double for the first month, as a way of saying thank you."

She knew she was promising a lot. This place was already way over-priced. But if she could just sell a few of her bubble baths to local stores, and get the money upfront, then she could turn this whole situation around.

The landlord licked his lips. "There are other ways to say thank you," he said, staring at Kiera's breasts. "Ways that I might just consider."

Kiera shuddered. She knew she'd been foolish to hope for a helping hand from the landlord, but she hadn't expected it to get this bad. "No," she said firmly. "I'm not going to do anything like that. But I promise you, you'll get your money—"

The landlord shrugged, his expression turning sour. "You're not listening to me," he said. "You either pay me upfront, in whatever creative ways that cute little body of yours can think of... or the deal's off." He grabbed his sweatpants, itching his crotch.

Kiera didn't dare look down, in case the disgusting man was hard already.

"My body's not a bargaining tool," she said, trying not to sound like the scared little thing she really was. "It's the money or nothing."

The landlord shrugged. "Shame. Bet you're into all kindsa kinky shit." He focused on the streak of blue in her hair now, as if that was an indicator of how sexually adventurous she was.

She stepped back, nauseated. "I have to go. If you change your mind about the money—"

He slammed the door shut in her face before she could say anything else.

Kiera stood outside on the sidewalk for a few minutes, trying to process what had just happened. She felt defeated and humiliated at the same time, but more than anything, she was determined not to let this be the end of her story.

Gathering her courage, Kiera took a deep breath.

"Never mind, Blinky," she said to the bear in her bag. "The day is young. The number of beauty stores in Miami is almost infinite. You got this."

But as the day wore on, Kiera knew that she did not have this. She did not have this *at all*.

And when day turned to night, Kiera finally accepted defeat, sitting down on the cold, hard streets with the misery of a reluctant woman dejectedly returning to an abusive partner.

*

Kiera shifted on the bench, trying to make herself comfortable.

It was almost impossible to sleep. She constantly had to keep one eye open, to check no one was coming for her or her stuff. She clutched Blinky as though her life depended on it.

If it wasn't someone coming to hurt her, it would be someone to arrest her. It was prohibited in Miami to camp, store personal belongings, or lie down on public property, including parks, sidewalks, and streets. If you got caught, you got fined or arrested.

Still, at least getting arrested meant you could get a warm cell for the night.

"There are worse places to be homeless than Downtown Miami, Kiera," she told herself. "It's warm, there are parks and beaches. Some of the rich people who pass through can be quite generous."

She'd been sleeping outside for over a week, and already, she was suffering the effects of sleep deprivation. She'd had palpitations, panic attacks, and she swore she'd even hallucinated a couple of times, seeing flashes of light in the corner of her eye, hearing faint sounds that seemed real, but only for a second.

Obviously, none of the bath and body stores she'd approached had been remotely interested, and the more time she'd spent on the streets, the more impossible it had become to try them. In fact, by day three of being homeless, she'd known that it was already too late. She'd started to smell bad, she looked dirty, and the products in her bag looked worn and strange. She felt like a kid trying to sell silly pretend potions to passers-by. It was time to stop living in make-believe land.

If Daisy's honeymoon hadn't been a six-week-long odyssey, she might have walked to her house by now. And she'd considered trying Peach's place too, but both of them lived in gated communities, so it was pretty obvious how that one would have played out.

She could have phoned them, but her phone had died and she had no way to charge it. She'd tried going into a coffee shop yesterday, but the seats next to the power sockets were taken by laptop-toting hipsters who stayed there for so long, she was kicked out for loitering. She tried going in again later on, but they told her she wasn't welcome back.

The truth was, Kiera had always felt a bit like she deserved this life. Like sooner or later, she was going to end up back here, because that was her destiny. She wasn't the sort of person who got to live in a multimillion-dollar mansion with a doting Daddy Dom. She wasn't a Daisy or a Peach. She was a Kiera. Homeless at fifteen. Addicted to painkillers and messed up from an early age.

In some ways, it was a relief to be back where she belonged. It was so tiring trying to pretend all the time.

Kiera sighed. She was so tired, so defeated.

But then, as if a sign from above, she heard the faint sound of a guitar. It was coming from the direction of the old train station, which had been converted into an outdoor market.

Kiera got off the bench and followed the sound, and eventually stopped in front of an elderly man, who was playing a soulful tune on his guitar.

She stood there for a few minutes, listening and enjoying the music, then politely clapped when he finished.

The old man smiled at her. "You like that song?"

She nodded. "Yes, it was beautiful. What's it called?"

He chuckled. "Oh, it's a traditional gospel tune. 'I'll Fly Away.'"

The old man began to play it again, and Kiera listened, mesmerized.

I'll fly away, she thought. *Maybe that's what I should do. Leave Miami. Hitchhike a ride back to Connecticut. Find all my old contacts. Get back on track.*

But even the thought of that exhausted her.

The man finished playing his tune and she wished that she could give him a coin or two. She started to clap again, but was distracted by a horrible smell on the early morning breeze.

"Oof," she said to him. "Those grilled onions smell horrible. They're turning my stomach."

"I can't smell anything," said the old man.

"Seriously?" said Kiera. "It's super strong."

She looked at the other end of the open-air market, and noticed the hot dog vendor setting up his station for the day. That was weird. Normally, she liked the smell of grilled onions. The hot dog stand was the whole reason she was camping out here, for the leftover hot dogs the man gave away at the end of the day.

"Woah, you can smell those onions from all the way over here?" the old man asked.

Kiera nodded, grimacing.

Then a thought hit her like a ton of bricks.

She remembered what Pauline had said when she'd walked into Bastion's mansion. Commenting on the smell of the cleaning products.

My nose is like a bloodhound's right now...

There was no way that she could be...?

Oh no. Kiera took birth control pills, or at least, she was meant to... but she wasn't always that good at remembering to take them. It would be very early days. But it was just possible that she could be...

That she could be...

Suddenly, as the panic rose in her, she threw up, all over the old man's feet.

Chapter Sixteen

BASTION

B ASTION HAD JUST COME out of a long business meeting with Sam from HR. Daddies Inc was doing so well that the company was having to hire twelve new members of staff.

He couldn't believe how far this company had come. It had seemed like such a pie-in-the-sky idea back when he, Montague, and Isaac had first dreamed it up. An exclusive club for Daddies and Littles, with partner companies all over the world. A secret DDlg room in the Hilton. Age play nights at the Moulin Rouge, treatments at the Canyon Ranch, fun weekends away at Santa Monica Beach. Daddies Inc had links with all manner of top-notch destinations all over the world. It was incredible to discover just how many people were into the age play community, whether they were fully immersed in the lifestyle, or just a little curious. Romance novels were a big factor. 'Daddy kink' books had sparked an interest in age play internationally, and now, Daddies Inc. was reaping the benefits.

Bastion should have been excited. He should have felt proud. But ever since Kiera had left him, he'd been deflated.

As Bastion walked across the parking lot, he wondered why he was even bothering going home. Not that he even had a home anymore.

For the last two weeks, he'd been staying at a hotel. Drinking from the minibar every goddamn night. Drinking, drinking, drinking. In spite of the promise he'd made to himself. In spite of the promise he'd made to Kiera.

What a fucking fool.

Tad was staying at the mansion with his mom with the new baby, who Pauline was *still* insisting was Bastion's. After Kiera left, Bastion had decided to let Pauline have it.

A huge decision.

A stupid decision.

And yet... he wanted Tad to have a good home. And Pauline had a newborn baby to consider, so...

Bastion had more than enough money to buy another mansion. Hell, he had enough money to buy ten mansions if he wanted to.

As soon as his removal people had taken his stuff out of the mansion, he'd start looking for somewhere. He just couldn't face it right now.

Not without Kiera.

Obviously, he'd been giving her space like she wanted. But it was hard. He'd hoped she would have reached out to him by now. Allowed him at least to explain things to her.

He'd tried getting Isaac to ask Peach how she was doing, but Isaac was busy at the ranch lately, and Bastion hadn't managed to get much out of him. Something about Kiera being away on a business trip, which sounded like nonsense to him. But the girl was entitled to her privacy if that's what she wanted.

As he put his key in the ignition, wondering whether to head back to the hotel yet or just drive to a bar, his phone rang.

Saved by the bell.

The second he picked up, Peach started blurting out frantic words. "Bastion. I think something's wrong. I haven't heard from Kiera in two weeks. She said she was going on a business trip slash vacation or something, but... I don't know. I had this weird dream about her, and I keep calling her phone, and I just feel like something's not right. I called Daisy on her honeymoon and she hasn't heard anything, either. Isaac said you'd been asking after her, and—"

Shit. Peach didn't know a thing about him and Kiera. And worse than that, she didn't know a thing about Kiera's whereabouts, either.

"Okay. Slow down, Peach. When did you last talk to her?"

"Just before she left, a couple of weeks ago," said Peach. "She said she was going to follow up on some business leads, but... she never talked to *you* about it, did she? I know she was working for you for a bit, so I was hoping—"

"I'm sorry," said Bastion. "She stopped working for me a couple of weeks ago. Where did she say she was headed?"

"Um, around Florida I think," said Peach. "She was kinda vague about it. Oh god, I'm such a bad friend. I've been so busy at the ranch, I forgot to check in with her and—"

"Leave it with me," said Bastion. "If you hear something, anything... call me right away."

Bastion hung up the phone and tried to think. His heart was racing.

What a selfish prick he'd been. Going about his life without calling her even once. Drinking in his hotel room. Feeling sorry for himself.

Think, Bastion.

He closed his eyes, trying to figure out where Kiera might be. It seemed unlikely that she had any business leads to follow up on. She'd have mentioned something like that to him. More likely, Kiera was in hiding somewhere. She had trouble asking anyone for help, and she had trust issues too.

So... could she have been back at her old apartment?

Maybe... but he knew for a fact that she didn't have any money. And unless her asshole landlord had let her stay there for free... His mind flipped through horrifying images of where she might be, what might have happened to her.

He looked around the parking lot, as if trying to find something, anything, to give him inspiration. And that's when he spotted something.

A hot dog restaurant across the street.

He remembered something Keira had said to him once. If she was ever homeless, she'd said, she'd go to the open-air market, where they gave away free hot dogs at the end of the day.

Well. It was an idea, at least. And he had to start somewhere.

He started driving toward the old train station, reminding himself not to speed.

By the time he pulled up near the open-air market, he was extremely worked up. With every heartbeat, his brain was screaming:

I'm such a fucking fool.

I'm such a fucking fool.

I'm such a fucking fool.

He hurried to the market, anxious and desperate. Even though it was late afternoon, the place was buzzing. Anyone and everyone seemed to have come here to hang out. Stoner kids, busy mothers with screaming babies, quiet retirees, flashy tourists, entwined lovers.

He searched for hours, feeling helpless. The smells from all the different food stalls were making him dizzy. Grilled meat. Roasting coffee. Fermented kimchi. Fragrant tagines. Spicy curries. It was all too much, too bright, too loud, for him to focus.

Obviously, he looked at all the hot dog places first. But none of them seemed to be giving away food for free, and of course, none of them led him to her.

"This was stupid," he muttered to himself. "You just don't know her very well, Bastion. You have no fucking clue where she is. Why are you even pretending?"

He turned to go back to his car, but as he did, he noticed a small, grubby-looking hot dog stand on the edge of the market that he hadn't noticed before. It had a long queue of people going down the street. And they weren't your ordinary people. They all looked... tattered. Run-down. Like baths were a luxury they couldn't afford. They were, most likely, homeless.

He strode over, his heart pounding in his throat.

Was she in the queue? Even if she wasn't, maybe the guy had seen her?

As he walked, an old guy played a gospel tune on his guitar on the street corner. A few people were singing along with him. He recognized the song as 'This Little Light of Mine.' Normally, Bastion might have appreciated something like that. Right now, though, he wished he could pay the guy to stop. The upbeat music was so jarring. It felt as though nobody should have the right to be so happy when...

Wait.

There was someone huddled on a step near the singer's feet. Poking out from under a hood, was a streak of hair. Blue.

"Kiera?" he called out, running over. The music had grown so loud he had to shout. "Kiera?"

When he was just a few steps away, the figure looked up, and Bastion saw that she was cuddling a pink teddy bear. Then he saw her face.

It was Kiera, but not as he remembered her. This Kiera was pale and clammy. She looked gaunt and somehow, barely present.

"Darling!" he said, sitting down beside her. "It's me, Bastion."

Kiera looked at him a frown playing on her exhausted face. "Daddy?"

Bastion felt relief flood through him. He had found her. but the relief was tempered by heavy concern. "Darling, we have to get you out of here. I need to help you."

"Daddy," she said, her teeth chattering, "I'm so c-cold."

Instantly, he pulled off his suit jacket and put it around Kiera's shoulders.

"Can you walk?" he asked her. "Or do you want me to carry you?"

Kiera didn't answer, so Bastion picked her up, horrified by how light she felt. How had she lost so much weight in just two weeks?

She wrapped her arms around his neck, nuzzling into him, and he started walking away.

As Bastion passed the gospel singer, he stopped playing his song for a moment.

"Take care of her," the singer said softly.

And then he continued.

"Come on, Kiera," Bastion said softly. "Let's get you some help."

"But... y-your baby," Kiera mumbled up at him.

"Not my baby," he told her. "I promise you."

Tears filled Kiera's eyes. "I'm h-homeless, Daddy."

"Not anymore, darling," he told her. "Not anymore."

"I have something to tell you, Daddy," she said softly. "Promise not to be angry?"

"Of course," he said, opening up his car and placing her down carefully on the passenger seat.

"I'm..." she began. "I'm..." Then, suddenly, she turned gray, and vomited all over the seats of his Bentley. "Oh no... your car..."

"I don't give a shit about my car," he said, and he meant it. "All I care about right now is you, Kiera. I love you."

"I..." Kiera began, and then she passed out.

*

Bastion paced the halls of the private hospital.

The hallway was long and white, and it seemed to stretch on for eternity. Even though this was the most expensive clinic in Miami, with tropical plants and contemporary oil paintings lining the hallway, Bastion felt like a prisoner, a man without hope. He walked in circles, around and around, a caged animal. His mind raced with all the possibilities, all the things that could be wrong with Kiera. His heart leaped up into his throat, and his stomach twisted into knots.

He glanced at the clock and saw that it had been nearly an hour since he'd been told to wait outside. He had no news and no idea what was happening. He felt so helpless and isolated. He had to do something to take his mind off the waiting.

He walked to the vending machine and bought a cup of coffee, then he sat down and tried to take a sip. It was too hot and tasted like ashes. It burned his tongue and he had to set it down. He closed his eyes and tried to relax, but his mind wouldn't stop racing.

He wished he had something stronger here to steady his nerves. For the past two weeks, he'd been drinking steadily but heavily. He felt shaky without a drink right now, like he was being forced to live in a reality he couldn't handle without alcohol. He wondered whether to slip away for a moment, to find a liquor store and acquire something stronger than coffee. He could feel the pull of the urge, like a gravitational force tempting him away.

But he knew he had to stay, no matter how long it took. As he had driven to the hospital, he had made a deal with himself. With God, even. He wasn't a religious man, but he'd done a lifetime's worth of praying on the way here. He had told God that if Kiera was okay, he would never drink again. And he had to keep his promise. He had to stay strong and hope for the best.

Just then, Doctor Ryker emerged from a door at the end of the hall. Bastion rushed to meet him, his stomach lurching. He looked into the doctor's face, desperate for news.

Dr. Ryker's expression was grim, but he said, "She's alright. We've stabilized her."

"Stabilized her?" Bastion asked. "From what?"

"She was severely dehydrated," said the doctor, "Plus, she had a urine infection, high blood pressure, and some bruising."

"Bruising?"

"I'd say it was consistent with her poor sleeping arrangements," said the doctor, "rather than the result of violence."

Even hearing that word, 'violence', made Bastion feel physically sick.

"But... none of that is life-threatening?" he asked the doctor, still having a hard time processing what he was hearing.

"Not to *her*, no," said the doctor.

Bastion looked into his eyes. "What do you mean?"

"Well, in her condition..." said the doctor, trailing off. He put his finger to his lips, as if he'd said too much.

"I'm sorry, I don't follow," said Bastion.

"I think it's best you talk to her," said Dr. Ryker. "Maybe you can help convince her to take painkillers for me. I have some perfectly safe ones, but she's refusing them."

"So, she's awake?"

"She is. Although she'll need plenty of rest."

Bastion thanked him and went to Kiera's room. She was lying in the bed, pale and still. She was hooked up to a variety of wires and tubes, with a drip of clear-colored liquid hanging above her, and a machine beeping softly to her left.

"Kiera?" he said gently. "How are you doing?"

He could see the worry in her eyes, and it hurt him so badly that the pain was almost physical. He brushed her hair away from her face and kissed her forehead.

She smiled weakly and said, "I'm okay, Daddy."

Bastion felt a tear escape his eyes. He sat beside her, holding her hand, and said, "I love you so much. I'm so relieved you're going to be okay."

Kiera nodded slowly.

"I'm going to take care of your every need when you leave this place," he told her. "You have nothing to worry about. Nothing at all."

"I don't know about that..." Kiera said softly. And then she started to cry.

"What's going on, babygirl?" he asked her. "Dr. Ryker says you're refusing pain medication. And he's also being very cryptic about what's going on with you. I really need some answers, babygirl—"

Slowly, Kiera lifted back the covers, and raised her hospital gown, revealing her thin body. Her ribs stuck out prominently, and he noticed some light bruising along one side. She took his hand and placed it below her navel.

"What's going on, darling?" he asked her. "Are you sick? Do you have a lump here? Are you—"

Kiera blinked at him, as though willing him to understand, and suddenly, he did.

Holy fuck.

"You're... pregnant?"

Kiera nodded. "It's still very early. Dr. Ryker says that my condition could make my body... inhospitable." She cried harder now, pushing away his hand and covering her face. "I'm sorry, Daddy. I was having so much fun with you that I forgot to take my birth control pill. And now I've totally messed up."

Bastion swallowed. Suddenly, it was like he was taking in every last detail. Of her. Of the room around him. Her beautiful eyes. The white clock. The slow, steady drip of the saline into her veins.

"Darling," he said to her, his words deep and true. "You're having our baby?"

Kiera nodded sadly.

"Dr. Ryker says I put the baby in a lot of danger while I was homeless, but if he monitors it carefully... Anyway, you don't have to be involved. It's my mistake."

Bastion's heart was doing somersaults. "Babygirl," he said, "this is no mistake. Not unless it feels that way to you. If this baby lives, I'm with you a hundred percent of the way. And if it doesn't, then I'm with you all the way, too. If you want me to be."

Kiera looked at him, confused. "You want to get back together?"

"Darling, I never wanted you to go," said Bastion. "I thought you wanted space, and if you still want it, then I respect that. If you don't want this baby, then I respect that too. But... I want you back in my life, Kiera. I need you."

Kiera bit her lip. "I need you too, Daddy."

"Then let me take care of you," said Bastion. Both of you."

Kiera smiled weakly. "So... can we go home now, Daddy?"

Bastion paused. "Slight problem," he said, giving Kiera a mock-serious look. "I don't actually have a home right now. So we're going to need to choose a new one. Together."

Kiera started to giggle. "You're homeless too? Oh, Daddy..."

Bastion rubbed her belly, hoping that the tiny child inside it would survive. Either way, something told him that things were going to work out okay for him and Kiera.

"Thought you said you weren't the giggly type," he teased Kiera.

She giggled some more. It was the most beautiful sound Bastion had ever heard.

Chapter Seventeen

KIERA

"I could get used to this," said Kiera, leaning back on her fluffy pillows and sighing contentedly.

She was staying at an even fancier hotel than the last one Bastion put her up in. It had all the trappings of a high-class establishment: velvet-cushioned chairs, expensively-framed art, a complimentary mini-bar full of milkshakes and smoothies as requested by Bastion, and fresh-cut flowers in every room. But what Kiera was most enjoying was the cartoon channel she could watch on the huge flat-screen TV.

Kiera and Bastion had been living in the hotel suite for a few days now, ever since she'd left the hospital. He'd set her up with a strict regimen of cartoons, room service, and relaxation, and he'd been true to his word. He'd even gone out and bought one of every toy in the local store, though they'd had to put half of them in storage because they didn't fit here.

They hadn't started looking at houses together yet, since Kiera was still regaining her strength, but it didn't matter. This was way too much fun.

"This is so much better than when I'm just homeless on my own," Kiera joked.

Bastion laughed. "I like to be homeless in style."

Bastion had explained why he had given Pauline the mansion, and she had expected to feel jealous, but she wasn't. Pauline had been essentially homeless too, and Kiera thought it was good of Bastion to be so selfless. It was important for Tad to have a stable home. Plus, she had to admit, after all those years of being homeless, it was thrilling to think that she'd have the opportunity to choose a house of her own. And not just any house. A freaking *mansion*!

Of course, there was still a ton of stuff she and Bastion needed to chat about, but Kiera was determined to work through it.

"The room service will be here any moment," Bastion told her. "Why don't you come and sit over here on the couch with me? The sunset is spectacular."

Kiera pretended to heave herself out of bed. She put on her dressing gown and walked over to the luxurious velvet couch that looked over at the most spectacular view of the Miami skyline and waters.

"You know, it's magical being here in this hotel with you, Daddy," she said, her voice wavering. "I still have to pinch myself when I think about where I was a week ago." She looked at Bastion in his expensive shirt and chinos, like someone straight out of a catalog. It was so hard to accept that she deserved this life. Especially since she'd put their baby in danger by making herself homeless. "Are you sure this is what you want? You don't feel... obliged?"

Bastion reached out for her. "Darling, I never wanted you gone in the first place. And the moment I got that call from Peach, I knew that

I was never letting you out of my sight again. That was before I even know about..." He looked down at Kiera's tummy. The two of them had tried not to talk about the baby too much, as if their words might jinx it, but it had clearly been on both of their minds a lot.

"I feel so silly for walking away from you," said Kiera. "I guess I just panicked when things got complicated. I put up my barriers like I always do... but I guess I'm realizing now that barriers don't always protect you. Sometimes, they just kinda get in the way."

Bastion nodded. "I understand why you did what you did. But you know, things are only as complicated as we choose to make them. I love you, you love me, we want to be together..."

Kiera smiled. "I think if you try to escape from every single complication in the world, you'll probably only end up making things more complicated."

"I prefer to think of complications as challenges," said Bastion, grinning. "Obstacles to climb over."

Just then, there was a knock at the door, and Bastion jumped over the side of the couch.

Moments later, he returned with a silver tray. Instantly, Kiera's mouth began to water.

"I still can't believe you want to eat this," said Bastion, handing her a bowl of vanilla ice-cream with cheesy nachos.

Kiera giggled. "I know."

Her sense of smell and taste seemed to have changed drastically almost the moment she became pregnant. She hated the thought of her previous favorite foods — pizza and hot dogs — and now, all she wanted was the strange mix of salty, sweet, and cheesy. It was a good thing that this fancy hotel was happy to make her whatever her strange heart desired.

"Think I'll stick to my Cuban sandwich," said Bastion, biting into his thick, toasted sandwich of ham, roast pork, Swiss cheese, and pickles. Yuck. The thought of a sandwich like that should have been delicious, but right now, it seemed as crazy as... ice-cream and nachos.

She looked out the window again, trying to focus on not vomiting. The sky was a canvas of gold and rose, painted by the setting sun that hung low over the horizon. The ocean glittered like a jewel, its waves a deep shade of blue that reflected the fading light. The beautiful view centered her.

"If you'd told me when I was fifteen that this would be my life," she said, taking a big spoonful of cheesy ice-cream, "then I'd have... well, it probably wouldn't have changed me much back then, but I'd have been a whole lot more excited about the future."

"Tell me more about your life back then," Bastion said gently. "I'd like to know about your past."

Kiera sighed. "Growing up, we never had much money, but my childhood was... okay. No brothers or sisters, and my parents always seemed to be working or arguing, but I never really had a problem with it. I was just a kid like any other, you know? Then, when I was thirteen, I was out riding a beat-up old bike I'd found and a man in an expensive car knocked me right off it." She winced, remembering the memory. "I hurt my back real bad and pretty much had to learn to walk again."

Bastion stopped eating his sandwich and took her hand in his. "Oh, Kiera. I'm so sorry."

"Obviously, my parents couldn't afford the medical bills. And the man in the expensive car seemed to get out of paying a dime. While my parents' debt grew higher and higher, I was stuck in bed, missing out on school and playing computer games. Plus, I was on this really strong medication, OxyContin." She felt her cheeks burning a fierce red. She had never admitted this to anyone.

"When my parents couldn't get it for me anymore, I couldn't handle it. I... started to find my own, through contacts I made on my gaming profile. I built up a secret stash. And then my parents found it and..."

She barely had the strength to finish the sentence. It was so painful, so exhausting, to open up like this. But she wanted to continue.

"They threatened to kick me out if I didn't stop. But... it wasn't that simple. I *couldn't* stop. So, they followed through and chucked me out when I was just fifteen."

Kiera could see Bastion's hands forming fists, his jaw tightening.

"I think they were probably relieved they didn't have to pay my bills anymore. I don't know how they dealt with me never going back to school, though. They should have been prosecuted with educational neglect charges, but as far as I know, they never were."

Kiera took a huge mouthful of ice-cream and then, with her mouth full and freezing, she said: "I... think I... hate them."

Bastion looked at her with an expression of deep kindness in her eyes. "I'm so sorry you had to go through all that," said Bastion. "And you have nothing to feel bad about. Parents have a duty to their children. Yours let you down."

Instantly, she felt the tension in her jaw and back muscles relax. It was okay to reveal herself to him. He was okay with it. She had nothing to hide anymore.

"I came off the drugs in the end," said Kiera. "Wasn't easy to stay on them while I was homeless. I hit rock bottom pretty quickly. Especially after this group of kids took all my stuff. But after I got cleaned up, I found work in a factory. Got paid almost nothing, in cash, no questions asked, but..."

"...it was something," Bastion said, filling in for her, showing her that he understood.

"Actually," said Kiera, "it was a soap factory. They gave me big boxes of free soap once in a while, and I vowed to never let myself get dirty ever again. And after making soap in the factory for over a year, I started getting ideas... about bubble bath."

Bastion smiled. "My resourceful girl."

"Anyway, pretty soon after that, I met Peach and Daisy in an ice-cream parlor, and the rest is history. They let me start my bubble bath business while I couch-surfed with them for a bit. I paid them in soap because I don't like charity, and soon, I managed to get a place of my own."

Bastion was looking at her intently, listening to every word. "I can't pretend to understand everything that you've lived through, darling, but I do know what it's like to be addicted to something. And I want you to know that me and alcohol are done now. No matter what."

Kiera smiled, unable to stifle yawned. "Oh man, I've been talking so much I've exhausted myself."

Bastion's face clouded with concern. "You need something? A massage? A bedtime story?"

She shook her head. "Just a nice big sleep, Daddy."

Bastion nodded. "Okay, but first we need to run you a bath. Especially after you vowed to never get dirty again." He sniffed her and pretended that she smelled bad, holding his nose.

She laughed loudly, pushing him playfully. "Hey, I'm not that bad!"

"Of course you're not, honey. But you know Daddy's rules: if you spend the day in bed, you have to take a bath and put new pajamas on at the end of the day."

Kiera finished her ice-cream while Bastion ran her a bath.

"Hey!" he called from the bathroom. "How about we use *your* bubble bath tonight? You still haven't shown me your collection."

Kiera felt awkward and embarrassed. She had talked up her bubble bath so much to Bastion, but the grubby products in her bag weren't impressive at all.

"I don't know..." she stalled. "The bottles look a mess now..."

"Sounds like someone's stalling," said Bastion, poking his head around the door. "Come on. I won't judge. Let's take a journey through the world of fragrances together!"

Kiera laughed. "You're silly."

"Silly, huh? Maybe I'll have to spank you for that later."

At the word "spank," Kiera felt her pussy tingle, and she hurried to go collect her bath products from the bedroom.

*

As Bastion stirred the last of the bubbles into the warm water, Kiera watched him, feeling warm and happy. The man of her dreams, who had made everything seem possible.

"Okay," said Bastion, "I have to level with you. I *love* the smell of this one. It reminds me of..." He bent down and sniffed the water. "It reminds me of the Fourth of July."

Kiera laughed. "It reminds you of Independence Day?"

"Sure," said Bastion, deadly serious. "I can smell apple pie, corn on the cob, and just a touch of barbecue smoke."

She considered this. "You know, that's actually pretty good. I call this one 'Pop Pop Bang Bang' because it's sour apple, cinnamon, and freshly roasted coffee. It's kinda based on the idea of a Sunday morning I always wished I could have. Curled up and cozy with some apple pie, coffee, and, er, well, you know, the man of my dreams." Blushing, she said, "Not sure where you got sweetcorn from, though."

Bastion knelt beside the bath, looking at her with tenderness in his eyes. "Darling, I would love to have that Sunday with you."

Kiera chewed her lower lip. "Um... shall we try the next one?"

"Sure," said Bastion, unscrewing the lid of the next bottle. "We won't add it to the bathwater or it'll all get mixed up, but let's take a hit." He put his nose over the bottle and gave it a long sniff. "Oh man. That's so good."

"It *is*?"

"This one's kinda like... a fun day at the movies?"

Kiera giggled wildly. "How do you get that?"

"Gummy worms... butter popcorn... red vines, maybe..."

"No way!" said Kiera. "Did you sneak a peek at the label?"

Bastion raised his palms. "No. I swear. Why did I get it?"

"Well, kinda... it's called 'Practical Joke Poke'!"

Bastion laughed. "It is?"

"Yeah, it's based on a practical joke I used to play on my school friends when I was a kid. Let's just say it involved gummy worms, butter, soil, and an empty matchbox."

Bastion looked both puzzled and amused. "Do I want to know?"

"I used to get people to poke their finger in the matchbox and see if they could guess what it was. Then, when they opened their eyes and saw the sticky worms covered in soil, they'd scream... hopefully."

Bastion shook his head. "You're something else, Kiera." He dipped his finger in the bath and then pressed a dollop of white foam onto her nose. "But I need to tell you something now. Something important. Your bubble baths smell amazing. Like, better than good. They combine nostalgia and fun scents and lighthearted names all at once. There's nothing wrong with your products. They're perfect."

Kiera's heart was racing and she was practically glowing. She'd been waiting so long to hear something like this. She just hoped that her Daddy wasn't lying to her.

"There is one problem, though," said Bastion.

Ah. Here it comes. The thing that would play over and over in her mind for the rest of time once she heard it. The dumb mistake she'd made. The reason she'd never succeed.

"The problem," he said, "is you haven't got *me* on board yet. You see, you're an inventor, Kiera. You're a dreamer. A product person. A genius. But... you're not a saleswoman. And thank god for that, or your product wouldn't be nearly as good. But me? I'm a salesman. Selling things is in my blood. Together, we'd make the perfect team. I can sell these products for you. If you want me to."

Kiera swallowed. "You're not just saying this to get in my bathwater?"

Bastion laughed. "I never lie about business."

Kiera reached up, grabbing her Daddy's face with sopping wet hands and kissing him. "Then... yes! Let's do it!"

Bastion smiled, obviously not caring how wet he was getting. And as they kissed, he started to undress. In less than a minute, he was in the water with her, and less than a minute after that, she was climaxing on his fingers, the scent of Independence Day all around them.

Chapter Eighteen

BASTION

Bastion and Kiera had spent the entire day looking at luxurious Miami mansions. Not one of the expensive homes had felt quite right. Now they were heading back to the hotel, and Bastion felt as though he'd failed his Little girl. The poor girl deserved a home more than just about anyone in the world.

"There was something to love about all of them," said Kiera. She sounded cheerful, but that wasn't enough. He wanted her to sound ecstatic. "Honestly, it's such a treat to look at all these expensive houses. I'm sure we could make any of them work."

"I don't care about making them work," said Bastion. "I care about making *you* sing. You deserve perfection."

Kiera smiled up at him. "Daddy, these houses are way beyond my wildest dreams. I mean, you know... they don't have jungle gyms in the basement or water slides or ball pits or inflatable bounce houses in the backyard, but... apart from that, they're *all* exactly what I always dreamed of. And anyway, I just want to be with you. Where we live, it's almost immaterial. As long as we're all together..."

Perhaps unthinkingly, she stroked her tummy. She was seven weeks pregnant now, and they had seen their little bean's heartbeat on a scan at the private hospital this morning. Bastion could see that Kiera's nausea was growing, but it was a healthy kind of nausea, not like the nasty, terrifying sickness she'd been suffering from when he had found her on the streets. This new sickness was kind of reassuring to them both. It told them that probably everything was still progressing as it should have been.

It amazed him, honestly, that he felt so sure that he wanted this baby. As much as he adored Tad, it had been difficult raising a child in an unhappy marriage. But then, he and Kiera weren't unhappy. She was his soulmate. And the idea of raising a child with her was just... exciting. Plus, knowing that there was a tiny piece of him growing inside her felt like the greatest gift a person could have. Especially after all those months of erectile dysfunction. He never dreamed something like this would be possible. He couldn't wait to see a bump start developing.

"You know," Kiera said, as they walked through the summer evening streets back toward their hotel, "I'd like to tell Peach and Daisy about us. And the baby."

Once Bastion had found Kiera, he'd let Peach know that she was okay, and that she was going to stay with him for a while, but he hadn't revealed any more than that. That was up to Kiera. Kiera had chatted to both her friends on the phone — Daisy was back from her honeymoon now — but she'd simply said that Bastion was looking after her and that she'd chat soon.

"I think that's a good plan," said Bastion. "Shall we invite them out to dinner tomorrow night and tell them then?"

Kiera squeezed his hand, a nervous look in her eyes. "Tomorrow? Yes, okay." She paused. "You know, when Peach and Isaac got together, I was so angry with Peach for keeping secrets from me. But I get it now. The need to protect the tiny kernel of a new relationship. Until it has a chance to grow and flourish in the outside world."

Bastion nodded. "It will be healthy to tell people about it now. To have a support network."

Kiera agreed. "There's so much to tell them, though. That we had a one-night stand at Daisy's wedding. That you're my Daddy now. That I rode your nice big cock so hard that you put a baby inside me."

Bastion's dick swelled slightly at the thought. They hadn't had sex since he'd found her because he was letting her recover, but he figured that she was probably about ready now. He'd been hoping they'd find the home of their dreams today, so they could celebrate.

"I'll make a reservation at the ice-cream and cheesy nacho place around the corner from us," Bastion joked.

"It's okay," said Kiera. "I could handle somewhere... relatively odorless." It wasn't *all* odors that bothered her. Just fried ones. And meaty ones. And bready ones. Bastion had stopped eating in the same room as her at the hotel, and tried to avoid mentioning any foods that weren't on her green list.

As they passed the harbor, Kiera took a long, deep sigh. "I just love this view," she said. "As long as our new house has this view, I'll be happy."

Bastion looked at the view too. Miami views were always spectacular, but there was something about the very spot where Kiera had stopped that spoke to him.

"You know what?" he said. "I've just had an idea."

Kiera turned to look at him. Her big eyes were two pools of curiosity. "You have?"

"This *is* going to be your view," he told her. He took hold of her by the shoulders, and turned her around one-eighty degrees, so that she was facing the opposite direction to the harbor. "Erm, that's not a house, Daddy. That's a patch of concrete."

Bastion bent down and whispered in her ear. "That's where you're wrong," he told her. "Keep looking harder."

Kiera laughed, screwing up her eyes. "Nope. Still concrete, Daddy."

Bastion ran over to the concrete and started waving his arms around excitedly as he walked around the empty space, speaking to her like a real estate agent.

"As you enter the mansion," he told her, pointing to a space on the left, "you are immediately greeted by a whimsical playroom filled with colorful toys, board games, and stuffed animals. A custom-built treehouse with slides and climbing ropes dominates the center of the room, while a giant indoor trampoline and a ball pit are located off to the side."

She frowned, confused, while still giggling.

"As you venture farther into the mansion," he continued, "you find a magical room with a massive indoor playground featuring a twisty slide, a rock-climbing wall, and a rope bridge. The room is decorated with a colorful mural featuring cartoon characters and giant lollipops."

Kiera put her hand to her mouth as he realized what he was saying. He was going to *build* her the house of his dreams.

"There is also a dedicated arts and crafts room, complete with a long worktable, art supplies, and a painting easel. The room is brightly lit, with large windows overlooking the lush backyard."

He ran to the back of the area of concrete.

"In the backyard, there's a large inflatable bounce house and an inflatable water slide set up for hours of outdoor fun. A playground with swings, slides, and a jungle gym is also located nearby."

Kiera ran over to him, looking at the area as though she could see everything he was talking about.

"For movie lovers," he continued, "there is a cozy cinema room with bean bag chairs, a popcorn machine, and a collection of classic Disney movies. You can also spend hours in the video game room, featuring the latest gaming consoles and a wall of TV screens. Overall, this imaginary mansion is the ultimate dream house for adults and children alike, with plenty of spaces to play, explore, and let your imagination run wild."

Kiera held onto Bastion's arm. "I think my imagination *is* running wild," she said. "But... can we really do it? Can we build our dream home?"

Bastion looked at her, his eyes wide and serious. "Yes," he told her. "In fact, it's exactly what we're going to do. And we're going to get the place built so fast we'll be in it long before the baby's born. There's only one thing I need to do before that happens."

Kiera slid her arms around him, nuzzling into him. "What's that, Daddy?"

Bastion pulled away from her, his heart racing. He reached into his pocket and pulled out a small blue box. Then, he got down on one knee and opened up the box.

"Kiera," he said, "babygirl, will you marry me?"

Kiera's cheeks streamed with tears. "Of course I will, Bastion," she said, sobbing and smiling. "You don't even need to ask."

"Oh, but I do," said Bastion, taking out the silver ring with an antique blue stone on it, and sliding it onto her finger. "Every day that I'm with you, I'll be asking what I did to deserve you, and what I can keep doing."

Kiera looked down at the ring. "I love it so much. And I love you."

"I spent a long time searching for a stone that matched the blue in your hair just right," he told her. "Wanted to make sure I got your favorite shade."

"You got it alright," she said, reaching up for his face and kissing him. "I just... thank you, Daddy."

Bastion's heart swelled with pride and happiness. "It's time to head back to the hotel," he told her. "But starting tomorrow, I'm going to find us temporary accommodation while we buy this land and build our house."

"What makes you so sure someone will sell you the land?" asked Kiera, gripping his hand as they walked.

"The billion dollars in my bank account makes me pretty damn sure," Bastion replied with a dry laugh. "Where there's a will there's a way."

Kiera clicked her tongue and shook her head. "You're naughty, Daddy. But I like it."

"You know, I have one more surprise in store for you back at the hotel," said Bastion. He had been nervous about the proposal. He had hoped that Kiera would have fallen in love with one of the houses today, and then he could have proposed there, but proposing to her on the spot of their future home felt very special too.

Now, though, he was even more nervous.

"Another surprise?" asked Kiera. "I hope you didn't buy me anything else. You'll spend all your money if you're not—"

"This way," said Bastion, dragging Kiera through the hotel reception and round to the left. Normally, they walked in the opposite direction, to the lobby that led to the elevators.

"Why are we going this way?" asked Kiera. "Wait. There's a sign saying the management is this way."

Bastion grinned down at her. "Follow me."

He led her into a meeting room where five important-looking men in gray business suits stood waiting to meet her.

"You must be Kiera Stark," said the one in the center, an older man with white hair, who Bastion knew was the CEO of the entire chain of hotels worldwide.

"Um, hi," said Kiera, casting a sideways look at Bastion. Her expression looked amused, scared, and eager to find out more, all at once.

"I'm Charles White," said the old man. "And I hope you've been enjoying your stay in my hotel."

"Oh!" said Kiera. "Yes. Very much so. It's extremely... posh."

The man smiled, his eyes sparkling. "Let me cut to the chase," he said, as one of the other men placed a silver tray containing multiple glass bottles on it. "Over the few days, we have all been testing out and enjoying your excellent range of bubble baths."

"Those aren't my..." Kiera replied, but Bastion squeezed her hand.

"I changed up the packaging," he whispered. "Hope you don't mind."

The man turned the glass bottles around and Kiera gasped. Bastion had gotten a graphic designer to design beautiful labels for the bottles, perfectly matching their personality, showing the fun, quirky products that they were.

"We want to stock these in our hotels across the world," said Charles White. "We'd like to stock this 'fun range' in our secret Little rooms, and the 'nostalgia range' in every other room... everywhere."

Kiera's jaw dropped. "Nostalgia range?"

"Yes," said Charles. "Bastion told us about the beautiful memories that the scents evoked. The Scottish highlands, a Connecticut lake, Miami Beach... We want you to create twelve nostalgia scents and then we want twelve fun ones, exclusively for use by our hotel." He slid a piece of paper across the table. "This is what we're offering initially, though of course that figure would rise substantially once the products were in use in every hotel across the world. We expect them to be fully rolled out within twelve months. By which time..." He slid across another piece of paper. "This is the annual contract figure."

Kiera looked as though she was having trouble speaking. Bastion hoped that was a good sign.

"We are very grateful for your offer," said Bastion. It was indeed a generous offer. Stupidly generous. But naturally, he'd get Isaac to look over the figures. "We will certainly consider it, won't we, Kiera?"

Kiera swallowed, her voice croaky and small. "Yes, it's... it's... it's a dream come true."

The men in suits laughed, and Kiera laughed too. In fact, she laughed so hard that Bastion eventually had to drag her out of the meeting, as happy tears rolled down her cheeks.

"Daddy," she said, "I don't know how you did that, but... thank you!"

"You did it," he said, grinning. "Maybe *you* can buy us that new house now," he joked.

As they walked up to their hotel room, Kiera said, "I hope there are no more surprises in store today. I'm not sure my heart could take it."

They entered their hotel room and Bastion closed the door behind them.

"So... your heart's too weak for surprises?" he asked, his voice low and deep.

Kiera turned to look at him, her eyes sparkling. "Why?"

He looked down at his crotch, then back at Kiera. "Guess I'd better make sure you have plenty of advance warning about what I'm about to do to you then, huh?"

Kiera licked her lips. "Uh-huh. I want to know everything."

"Well," said Bastion, "in around sixty seconds, I'm going to unzip my fly and show you the raging hard boner in my pants."

"Mmm-hmmm," said Kiera.

"Then you're going to get down on your hands and knees, and crawl over to me with your mouth wide open."

"Mm-kay," Kiera whispered.

"You're going to suck your daddy's cock like it's the most delicious ice-cream you ever ate. And when Daddy decides you've been a very good girl and you've sucked his cock for long enough, he's going to get you to crawl over to the bed and hold onto the headboard, so that you can admire your lovely new engagement ring while Daddy enters your pussy from behind. Then, he's going to fuck you harder than he's ever fucked you before, while you tell him what a good Daddy he's been today. Understood?"

Kiera smiled and nodded. "Yes, sir."

"Good," said Bastion. His cock had been hard all day on and off, but rattling through that speech just now had made it harder than the sapphire on Kiera's engagement ring.

He unzipped his pants, and he didn't even need to pull his cock out — it sprang out of its own accord, ready to be admired, licked, sucked.

Kiera immediately dropped to her knees, then, slowly, she crawled over to him. This part was risky, as he knew how delicate her stomach was, but he hoped that thinking of his dick as an ice-cream would help with her nausea.

Clearly, the magic worked, because Kiera kneeled before him with a big smile on her face, then she reached up for his cock and stuck it down the back of her throat as though it was the most wonderful thing she'd eaten in weeks.

"Good girl," Bastion said soothingly. "That's just how Daddy likes it. Don't be afraid to bite him gently now and then."

Kiera did as he asked, gently sinking her teeth into his juicy girth, and it drove him to the edge of desire.

"Holy fuck, babygirl," he panted. "You're so right for me."

He grabbed hold of her hair to steady himself, trying his hardest to think of unsexy things: cabbages, doormats, trashcans. It didn't work, though. His dick swelled and throbbed and he knew that he was in danger of coming any moment.

"Shit," he said urgently, pulling out his dick, which was dripping wet with her spit. "You've been a very good girl. Now get over to that bed."

Kiera turned around and obediently crawled over to the bed, swaying her ass slightly as she crawled. Then, she climbed into the mattress and held onto the headboard.

Bastion got behind her and yanked down her pants and panties. Her beautiful ass shone in the evening light, and he felt tempted to guide his erection right between those two round white cheeks.

But that wasn't what he'd promised. And it wasn't what he was desperate for, either. Tonight, right now, he wanted to fill up Kiera's pussy with his seed. She was his fiancee, after all. He wanted to consecrate the memory with a holy fucking climax deep inside her sacred hole.

As Kiera's knuckles gripped the wooden headboard, he took hold of his thick shaft and found her soft, moist pussy lips with his hungry tip. He didn't need to squeeze or push to get inside of her — she was so wet and open for him that he slid all the way in, deep and satisfying.

"Damn, babygirl," he said. "You were ready for Daddy, huh?"

"I've been ready for days, Daddy," she said, pushing back onto his hard dick, letting him get as deep as humanly possible.

"Then hold on tight," he instructed her. "Daddy's not going to hold back today."

Kiera clasped the headboard with all her might, and he fucked her from behind like an animal possessed. He was a wolf, he was a bear, he was a man who had finally got everything he wanted, and he was never, ever going to let it out of his sight.

"Daddy's gonna fill you up now, Little one," he said, when he felt himself about to burst. Then, as his cock raged and erupted inside of her, his mind finally grew quiet and clear. He pulled out over her, flipping her over onto her back, and kissing her stomach, then her mouth.

Kiera smiled sleepily at him. "That was good, Daddy," she said. "I like it rough."

Bastion bent down at bit her shoulder, so hard it made her squeal. He left a bite mark, but no blood. "Careful what you wish for," he said sternly.

Kiera looked taken aback for a moment, then she grabbed hold of his shoulder and bit him back.

Damn, that felt good.

"Harder, babygirl," he said. "Bite as hard as you can."

Kiera sunk her teeth into his skin so hard that he felt a tingle of pleasure in his groin.

"Looks like round two's coming quicker than you thought," he said, rubbing his hardening cock between her legs.

Kiera opened her thighs wider, letting him rub himself wherever he goddamn pleased, until within a matter of minutes, he was ready to fuck her tight little body all over again, in whichever hole he felt like.

After all, she belonged to him now. Not just as his future wife, not just as his Little, not just as his business partner or housemate or the mother of his child. She was all of those things, but right now, she was his submissive, and he and his recently fixed dick had some deep, dominant fucking to do.

So, he pushed her onto her side, parted her ass cheeks, and squeezed his dick deep inside of her...

Chapter Nineteen

KIERA

K IERA SMILED AS SHE looked at her two best friends, Peach and Daisy.

"Thank you so much for throwing me this party," she said, as the three of them lay back in the bubbly jacuzzi.

"Are you kidding?" said Daisy. "We wouldn't have let you get married without a bachelorette party."

"Plus we get to hang out all day at a spa," said Peach. "Got to make the most of this before I give birth!"

Peach was nine months pregnant now, and she was having triplets. The skin of her stomach looked so stretched it scared Kiera a little to think hers might do that soon enough. Peach seemed comfortable with the idea of carrying three children around inside her. Kiera was glad she was only having one.

Only six weeks ago, Kiera had come clean to her friends about her relationship with Bastion. She'd told them about the outfit he'd made her clean his house in. She'd told them about the butt plug and even the diapers. She'd told them about Tad and Pauline.

But she hadn't yet told them about the pregnancy. Until now, it had felt a little premature. She wanted to make sure that the pregnancy was progressing okay first. Plus, she didn't want to steal Peach's limelight. Peach was in full-blown baby mode. Isaac was making her eat six small but nutritious meals a day to feed the babies inside her, and she was fat and happy as a person could be.

But now, as they all lounged around together in bikinis, Kiera felt like it was hard to keep her secret any longer.

"There's something else I need to tell you," said Kiera, rubbing her tummy. She hadn't felt any kicks yet, but the expensive doula Bastion had hired for her told her that it might happen over the next few weeks.

"More secrets?" said Peach, raising an eyebrow and grinning.

Her friends hadn't actually been angry with her at all about keeping Bastion a secret. They'd both recently gotten with their Daddies, and although there had been some issues when Peach and Isaac got together, the friends had worked through them, and they understood now that sometimes, people needed their privacy.

What they weren't so impressed with was the fact that Kiera hadn't asked them for help when she became homeless. They told her that her pride must never get in the way of her health again, and she agreed. Especially now that she was to become a mother...

"I... I'm actually p-pregnant," Kiera said, so quietly her friends could barely hear her over the bubbles.

Suddenly, Daisy started to laugh. "I'm so glad you told us," she said. "I thought maybe Bastion was feeding you too many high-calorie baby foods."

It was true that Bastion had been feeding her baby food. It had felt a little embarrassing at first, but he had suggested it because of her nausea: baby food tasted so mild and was so easy on the digestive system. And it had turned out that Kiera loved it so much she demanded it for every meal. Mashed sweet potatoes. Mashed corn. Mashed pear and apple. She ate in the hotel room with her sippy cup and bib, and she even let Bastion diaper her at night since she needed to pee all the time now that she was pregnant, and he didn't like her having to get up too many times in the night or she got too tired the next day.

Yes, he had regressed her, but... yes, she liked it.

Becoming a mother was a scary business, and it felt good to be able to be Bastion's Little girl from time to time, reminding her that their relationship dynamic didn't have to change just because they had a child on the way.

"Oh my goodness! Congratulations!" said Peach. "That's so exciting! When are you due? Our babies can be friends!"

"Not for another five and a half months," said Kiera. "We don't even know if it'll be a boy or a girl yet. But there's definitely only one in there."

"How does Tad feel about it?" asked Peach kindly.

Kiera gritted her teeth. "Tad doesn't know yet. He's still getting used to the idea of Bastion and me... I think he's maybe freaked out by his dad being with a younger woman."

"From the sounds of it, maybe he had a little crush on you when you first met?"

Kiera blushed. "Maybe. Anyway, we'll tell him soon. I'll take Bastion's lead on that."

"Well, don't worry about that right now," said Daisy. "We're at a spa, and it's the most luxurious spa I've ever been to. Hydrotherapy, cryotherapy, gold-infused skincare products..." She laughed. "It's not so bad having billionaire Daddies, eh girls?"

Kiera and Peach both laughed.

"Seriously, though," said Daisy. "It's so exciting you're marrying Bastion! So tell us, what's he like as a Daddy? I always thought he'd be super scary."

Now that she had recovered from her illness, Bastion had become a little more stern with her. He spanked her over his knee a couple times a week, although, in the last few days, her tummy had gotten a bit bigger, so he'd started spanking her while she stood in the naughty corner of their hotel room. He was quite creative with his punishments too. Making her write lines on the hotel notepaper, making her walk around the hotel room naked all day while he worked, making her suck his cock for an hour while he replied to his emails, then coming on her breasts, coming on her face, coming on her ass...

Now that his impotence was cured, he was an unstoppable sex machine.

Kiera smiled. "He's not that bad, once you get to know him."

*

"You doing okay?" asked Bastion.

Kiera nodded. "Yes, Daddy," she whispered. "I'm excited."

But her heart was racing in anticipation as they walked through the hospital doors. What would they see on the ultrasound? Would the baby be okay? Would it be a boy or a girl?

They were back at the expensive hospital, where Bastion paid for all of Kiera's treatment, and the ultrasound technician was incredibly gentle and patient with them. She took her time to explain the procedure and made sure that Kiera was comfortable before starting.

As she rubbed the jelly on Kiera's abdomen, and then placed the probe down on her tiny bump, she smiled immediately. "Baby's doing great today," she said. "So... do you want to know the gender?"

Kiera looked at Bastion. They'd talked about the sex of their baby a lot, and agreed that it didn't matter either way, but Kiera knew what she was secretly hoping for.

"We do," said Bastion, squeezing Kiera's hand.

As the technician announced: "It's a girl!", Kiera's eyes filled with tears.

"Oh my god," said Bastion. "My babygirl is giving me a daughter."

Kiera laughed happily. A girl had been her secret wish. Perhaps because Bastion already had a boy, and she wanted to feel as though she'd given him something different.

"Darling," he said, kissing her. "I'm so happy." He bent down and whispered in her ear: "I wish I could fuck you in here, right now. Use all that jelly on your belly as lubricant."

Kiera blushed and they thanked the technician for her time and left.

As they walked down the corridor, Kiera felt giddy. "We should celebrate," she said. "Our baby is okay. *She* is okay."

Bastion put his arm around Kiera. "We will celebrate, darling. We'll do whatever you want. But first... there's something we need to do. We need to talk to Tad."

Kiera grimaced. "Right now?"

She hated the thought of Tad taking it badly, and as soon as Tad found out, it was only a matter of time before Pauline found out. Pauline had her own baby, obviously: a girl called Lily. Lily had dark skin and looked nothing like Bastion, but Pauline was still maintaining that the baby was his. Kiera trusted Bastion and knew that he was telling the truth, though. She got the feeling that Pauline might be jealous that she was carrying Bastion's actual baby inside her.

"Come on," said Bastion. "It's like ripping off a Band-Aid. I'll buy you all the baby food you can eat after."

Kiera took a deep breath. "Can we go to the adult soft play too?"

"You bet your ass we can," said Bastion. "Then Daddy's taking you to the building site to go check on our new home. And if nobody's around, Daddy's fucking you in the place where our new bedroom will be."

Kiera felt her cheeks flush with excitement. "Okay, Daddy," she said. "Let's go rip off the Band-Aid."

Chapter Twenty

BASTION

B ASTION, KIERA, AND TAD arrived at the baseball game late in
the afternoon. The sun was setting, casting an orange glow over
the stadium and the surrounding city. People were streaming in and
out, their faces alight with anticipation. They'd been lucky to get these
tickets at the last minute.

Tad, who was not much of a sports fan, was not particularly excited.
"I don't see why you brought me here," he moaned. "I'd rather stay at
home and play Final Fantasy."

Bastion gritted his teeth together. "This is something that we can all
enjoy together," he told his son. "Out in the fresh air, with the noise
and the smells of the stadium around us. You'll love it. I promise."

Bastion hoped he was right. As a young boy, he and his dad had
bonded over trips to baseball games. Now that his father was no longer
around, he hoped to relive some of that happiness with his son. But it
was so hard to peel Tad away from a computer screen.

Tad sighed. "Fine."

Bastion cast a sideways look at Kiera. She was obviously nervous,
and he hoped the smell of fried food wasn't too much for her. He
hoped he was right about how this would bring them all together.

As they took their seats in a private box, Bastion tried to get Tad excited about the game. He described the history of the team they were rooting for: the Miami Marlins. He talked about the rivalries between the Marlins and the New York Mets, as well as describing some of the key players: Jazz Chisholm Junior, a young second baseman with his flashy play and charismatic personality, and Sandy Alcantara, who had a fastball that could reach over a hundred miles an hour.

Tad looked increasingly interested as the conversation went on. "So, like, the players have stats and stuff? A bit like in Final Fantasy?"

"Yes," said Bastion, laughing. "Just like in your computer game."

Just then, the waiter came up to them and asked if they'd like anything to eat or drink. Here in the private box, they could order any of the upscale food and drink options they liked: sushi, craft beer, chili.

"They have nachos here," he whispered to Kiera.

"No, it's okay," she said, smiling brightly. "I actually feel like a hot dog today!"

Bastion felt a thrill of happiness run through him. She was feeling a little better, starting to move toward that more comfortable second trimester people talked about.

"Ooh, I'll have the same as Kiera," said Tad, licking his lips.

"Three hot dogs, then!" said Bastion, clapping his hands together.

They looked around the stadium, enjoying the lively atmosphere. This place, LoanDepot Park, had a unique design with a retractable roof and large glass panels providing views of downtown Miami. Bastion could see the market where he'd picked up Kiera from here. How incredible to think that if he hadn't found her, she might still have been down there. How fucking scary.

He squeezed Kiera's hand. "I love you," he whispered in her ear.

"Woah," Tad said, distracted by something. "That video board is huge. Will we get to watch the whole thing in high definition?"

Bastion laughed again. "Yes, son, we will."

"Here you go, sir," said the server, returning with the hot dogs. "Would you like mustard?"

"I'll have a little," said Kiera brightly.

"I'll have a ton," said Tad.

"Fine, I'll have a ton and a half," said Kiera, giggling.

Bastion watched his son and his fiancee joking around with a happy heart. This was what it was all about. The family life he'd always dreamed of. He just hoped the news that he and Kiera were revealing to Tad would be well received.

"Settle down now," said Bastion. "Looks like the game's about to start."

The Marlins were playing the Tampa Bay Rays, another of their rivals, and the game started with a bang. The Rays center fielder, Kevin Kiermaier, led off with a solo home run off Marlins starter Sandy Alcantara. The Rays kept the pressure on, tacking on two more runs in the second inning with RBI hits by Brandon Lowe and Manuel Margot.

But the Marlins weren't ready to back down yet. They answered back in the bottom of the second with a solo shot of their own, courtesy of outfielder Starling Marte. The Marlins kept chipping away at the Rays' lead, scoring another run in the fourth inning on a sacrifice fly by first baseman Jesus Aguilar.

Every time the Marlins scored a run, Tad and Kiera cheered and waved their arms around wildly. By the time the first half of the game was over, even though the Rays held a one-run lead over the Marlins, Kiera and Tad looked full to the brim with delight.

"Dad, this is so exciting," said Tad, turning to Bastion.

"It really is," Kiera agreed. "I never knew I was a sports fan!"

Bastion grinned. "I had a hunch."

The plan had been to reveal the news about the baby to Tad after the game, but he just couldn't hold it in any longer. He gave Kiera a serious look, and she nodded, her big dark eyes blinking at him, full of love and trust.

Bastion put his arm around Tad's shoulders and said, "Tad, I need to tell you something..."

Tad leaned in to listen. "Yes, Dad?"

Bastion took a deep breath and said, "Kiera is pregnant. We're going to have a baby."

It took a moment for the words to sink in. Tad stared at Bastion blankly.

Kiera smiled at Tad, her eyes welling up with tears. "It's true," she said softly. "Your dad and I are going to have a baby."

Tad blinked rapidly, trying to process this new information. It had been a shock to him to learn that his dad was getting married, but this was obviously a far greater shock. "So... you got Mom and Kiera pregnant at the same time?"

Poor kid. Pauline was filling his brain with such nonsense.

"Actually, no," Bastion replied swiftly. "Just Kiera. I don't know who Lily's father is. I'm sorry. I keep asking your mother to tell you the truth. I'll order a DNA test to prove it to you if I have to."

Tad rubbed his head, frowning. "Well, there's a guy called Roberto who keeps coming round to ours. Mom says he's the interior designer. Doesn't look much like an interior designer. And they keep going to check out the... bedroom." He blushed as the penny dropped. "Oh. Do you think *he's* the father?"

"Looks like we all need a chat with your mom," said Bastion. "Are you okay with that? If we do it after the game?"

Tad nodded. "I guess... I was just kinda hoping we could hang out all day..."

Bastion glanced at Kiera. He'd promised her a session at the adult soft play center after this, followed by some baby food, and a steamy trip to the building site of their future home. But Kiera was nodding at him enthusiastically now, letting him know that the change in plan worked for her. He made a mental note to reward her for her generosity very soon.

"You can stay with us the whole weekend if you like," said Bastion. "If you feel ready…"

They were still staying at the hotel while the house was being finished, but Bastion could easily book an apartment for them to stay in over the weekend. In fact, fuck it. They could all go away somewhere for the rest of the weekend. But only if Tad was alright with all this.

"I guess I'm ready," Tad said. "I like spending time with you both." He looked at Kiera. "So… are you having a girl or a boy?"

"A girl," said Kiera shyly.

Tad swallowed. "Another half-sister."

"Bastion and I were thinking… maybe you'd like to give her a middle name?"

"Really?" asked Tad, the emotion showing in his voice. "You'd let me do that?"

Kiera nodded, smiling, her eyes full of tears. "Of course. You're part of our family. We love you, Tad."

Tad smiled and then burst into tears. "I missed you, Dad. I'm sorry for cussing at you."

The three of them embraced, and Bastion sighed with relief.

Tad knew the truth.

You could start building anything as long as you laid the right foundations.

*

"Well," said Bastion, "here we are."

As he parked his Bentley outside his old mansion, he felt a spike of nostalgia. This was the house he'd lived in when Tad was born. The house he'd gotten to know Kiera in.

Still, it was time to move on, and he was glad of it. That house was so... full of glass. Pauline's idea originally, not his. At the time, he'd been into it. Glass was shiny when it was new... but it soon got dirty, full of grime and fingerprints. You spent your whole day looking at your own reflection in it, and if it ever broke, it could cut you so deep you bled.

He was glad to be free of it.

His home with Kiera was going to be completely different. Open plan. Hardly any walls. Soft furnishings. Bright colors and patterns. Essentially, it was going to be so much more fun. And Tad was going to love staying there with them.

"Are you sure you want me to come inside?" Kiera asked, still in the car with her seatbelt on. "Maybe I should stay here while you two... clear the air."

"No," said Bastion firmly. "We're family. We stick together."

Kiera nodded, getting out of the car.

Bastion noticed the small bump under Kiera's *Teenage Mutant Ninja Turtles* t-shirt. It was cute to see her starting to show in public. He couldn't wait until the bump got even bigger and everyone who saw them out together would know that he, Bastion Barclay, had gotten this beautiful young woman pregnant.

Bastion and Kiera walked to the house, hand in hand, as Tad led the way.

"I hope Mom tells me the truth," Tad said, turning to Bastion, "about Lily."

As they entered the house, Tad called out for Pauline. Bastion noticed that she had already changed a lot of stuff in here. There was even more glass than before, for one thing. Plus, there was a lot of very flowery wallpaper and fragile-looking crystal ornaments. It wasn't Bastion's style at all. Strange to think that he had ever been with someone with Pauline's preferences.

Bastion had always been into a classic vintage look. He and Kiera had talked about how to blend their tastes — her love of bright and punky modernism, and his love of dark wood and leather-bound books. They'd decided they wouldn't even bother trying to blend them. They'd just go for a mixture of whatever either of them liked. Mahogany writing bureaus, rainbow-colored rugs, leather armchairs, and Andy Warhol prints. Who cared if it clashed? Bastion looked forward to the eclectic life they'd create in their new home. It would be a good sort of messy, not like his old life which had just been... a bad sort.

"Mom!" Tad called again. "Mom, where are you? I need to talk to you."

Pauline appeared at the top of the stairs. Her blond hair was tied in a messy bun, and she was wearing pajamas. She looked... exhausted.

"What's he doing here?" asked Pauline, looking at Bastion warily. "And what's *she* doing here?"

"They've come to talk," said Tad, leading Bastion and Kiera over to the newly-reconfigured seating area by the kitchen. Bastion had never seen a glass couch before, but... here he was, sitting down on it.

Note to self: glass couch equals ouch.

Pauline came down the stairs, glancing behind her awkwardly. "It's, uh, Lily's naptime," she said. "So don't be too loud, please."

"Dad has something to tell you," said Tad.

Bastion felt so proud of his son, stepping up to the plate and acting like the young man he was growing into.

Pauline sat down on a beanbag near them. How come she got to sit on a comfy beanbag, while he and his pregnant fiancée had to sit down on this glass monstrosity?

"I already know about the engagement," said Pauline moodily, "if that's what you're here to tell me."

"There's more to discuss," said Bastion, his voice deep and confident. He wanted to let Kiera know that this conversation didn't scare him. In fact, it was vital that it happened. "My future wife, Kiera, is pregnant."

Pauline's jaw dropped, and her gaze fell to Kiera's stomach. "Already?"

"Yes," said Bastion softly. "Already."

"But... you said that you never wanted another... with me..."

That's because you lied and cheated and made our married life a misery.

"She's due in around five months," Bastion continued. "We wanted you to know as early as we felt comfortable sharing the news."

Pauline scowled as she took the news in. "So, you did it," Pauline said to Kiera. "You stole my husband and his sperm."

Tad grimaced.

Kiera's face turned crimson. "I... you two weren't together when we..."

"It's okay, Kiera," said Bastion, squeezing her hand. "Nobody stole anybody. You and I were already living apart, Pauline. We were already divorced."

"But she's so... young," said Pauline, a horrified look on her face.

"She's over twenty-one," said Bastion. "It's perfectly legal."

As Pauline's face struggled to stay still, Tad spoke to his mother gently. "Mom," he said, "who is Lily's father? I don't believe you when you say that she's Dad's."

Pauline glanced upstairs again. "She's, um..."

Just then, they all heard the creak of a floorboard at the top of the stairs, and Bastion turned around to look. Standing there was a very overweight man, with a hairy belly. He was naked, except for a towel.

"Pauline, baby!" he called. "Are you coming back to—"

That's when he noticed the guests, and immediately, he took a step back. "Oh. I'm so sorry. Shit, Pauline."

Pauline took a deep breath, composing herself. "It's okay, Roberto," she called. "You may as well come down."

Roberto looked down at his belly and then shrugged. "Alright," he said. "If that's what you want."

Roberto hovered awkwardly next to the beanbag, and Pauline threw a blanket from the couch over him.

Gratefully, he wrapped himself up in it, then said: "Tad. Good to see you, my main man. We thought you'd be out at the game all afternoon."

Tad made a small grunting noise.

"Tad, darling, this is Roberto," said Pauline. "He's our interior designer... and my lover."

Bastion suddenly realized that he recognized this man. He'd seen him on a list of the richest men in Miami. He was wealthy as hell. Yes, Bastion was loaded too, but this man liked to splash out on superyachts and nightclubs all around town.

"Is he Lily's dad?" asked Tad warily.

Pauline paused. "No, honey. He's not. I... don't know who Lily's dad is. I've been so ashamed to admit that to you. I just... don't know. I guess I hoped that she was your dad's since we were still living together, but I think… realistically…" She sniffed. "I thought at first it was Ezra's. But Ezra did a paternity test. And when he found out he wasn't the father…"

Pauline stopped talking and looked up at Roberto apologetically.

Roberto's eyebrows were raised. He was clearly hearing this for the first time, but, to give him credit, he put his hand on Pauline's shoulder supportively.

"It's okay, Pauline," he told her. "It's good you've told the truth. And I will help you raise your girl, if you want me to."

"You will?" asked Pauline, crying a little.

"Of course," said Roberto, lifting her up off the beanbag and wrapping her inside the throw with him. They kissed, a little too passionately, as though they had forgotten they had company, then Pauline pulled away.

"Tad, I'm so sorry, darling."

Tad stared at her. "I just want everyone to tell me the truth. I can handle it. I'm not a kid anymore."

Pauline looked at Bastion. "I… I'm sorry I poisoned Tad against you," she said. "I just didn't want to lose him."

She walked over to Tad and threw her arms around him, kissing his cheek so hard he screwed his eyes shut.

"Mom! Quit it!"

"I love you, little man," she said. Then, she looked at Bastion. "You know, I need to move on from us. I'm happy with Roberto. I'm just… jealous of *her* youth." He pointed at Kiera. "And I'm jealous that I could never find a way to love you."

"I can buy you all the youth potions you want, my dear," Roberto said behind her. "Besides, you look perfecto to me."

Bastion felt happy for Pauline that this man seemed so loyal to her. And he felt even happier that Tad and Kiera were here to see the truth play out. Hopefully, they could all start to heal their wounds soon.

"Mom," said Tad. "There's something I want to ask you. I love staying here with you, but... I want to see more of Dad and Kiera too. I'd like to stay with them more than just every other weekend." He turned to Bastion. "If that's okay with you, Dad? And with Kiera?"

Bastion looked at Kiera and the two of them nodded at Tad. "We'd love that."

"Wait until you see our new games room," said Kiera.

"So, will you spend the rest of the weekend with us, Tad? We'll take you on a magical mystery tour. Starting with the building site for our new house, and then... wherever the wind blows us."

"Alright, Dad," said Tad, smiling. "Come on, then."

"See you on Monday after school!" Pauline called after them as they left.

"See ya, Mom!" called Tad. For the first time in ages, Tad looked as though a weight had been lifted from his shoulders, and he could breathe again.

Kiera looked happy too.

"I love you," Bastion whispered to her.

She pulled on his hand, standing on tiptoes as she whispered into his ear. "I love you too, Daddy."

Chapter Twenty-One

KIERA

T HE SECOND TRIMESTER WAS in full swing. A time for plump rosy cheeks, nesting, and... wearing a butt plug while your Daddy spanks you silly for spilling bubble bath all over your brand-new kitchen.

"But I thought you said I didn't have to be such a clean freak anymore!" squealed Kiera, giggling as Bastion chased her around the kitchen, brandishing the butt plug at her.

Bastion laughed. "Come here, you naughty sausage." He grabbed hold of her and gently pushed her down over the kitchen counter.

Everything about their new house was amazing, including the marble worktops. The only glass was in the windows and cups, and everything downstairs had been kept as open-plan as possible. They had both agreed that they didn't want to build too many barriers between them. Life was about being connected, after all.

Kiera's heavy, already milky breasts squashed against the counter, but he was careful not to push her stomach into it. "There's taking it easy with the cleaning and then there's being a messy little miss," he told her. "Now be a good girl and stop squirming."

Kiera felt Bastion pulling down her elasticated diaper, and then she felt the cool, lubricated tip of the anal plug entering her asshole. But there was more. This butt plug was new, and it was unlike any of the others Bastion had used on her. This one was U-shaped, with a long-thick tip that entered her pussy at the same time.

"That's it," he said, as he began pushing it in. "Take your punishment like a good girl for Daddy."

Kiera felt the diaper fall down to her ankles, and she stuck her ass out all the way so Bastion could get the plug as deep into both holes as possible.

"Holy sh... sheets, Daddy," she said, her teeth chattering.

"Does that feel good, babygirl?" Bastion asked her.

"Y-yes," said Kiera, unable to keep her hips still. She ground her butt back into Bastion, but he stopped her.

"Bad girl," he said. "Did Daddy say you could rub your pussy and butt on him? Daddy's wearing his work clothes. Daddy doesn't want your pussy juice all over his smart pants, now, does he?"

"Sorry, sir," said Kiera. "I'll behave."

"Glad to hear it," said Bastion. "Stay still while I spank you, then. Five spanks for spilling bubble bath on the kitchen floor, and five spanks for rubbing your pussy on me."

Kiera braced herself. "Okay, Daddy."

Bastion didn't waste another second before bringing his hand down on her ass. The moment his palm made contact with her, it made the double-ended plug jolt inside her, sending waves of pleasure around every inch of her body.

"Don't you dare come while I'm spanking you," warned Bastion, "or you'll be punished."

Kiera bit her lip, trying to hide her moans and pleasure, but she could feel her moisture trickling down her legs, more and more of it with every hard slap.

"Three more," Bastion growled in her ear. "Remember: no coming."

Kiera screwed her eyes tight shut. She tensed her body and begged it with every fiber of her being not to come. But she was a horny, horny pregnant woman, and her pussy and asshole were being stretched open and probed by a thick double-ended dildo, and her Daddy was spanking her extra hard, and...

"Oops."

The word escaped her lips at the very moment that her knees gave way, and she shuddered and shook on the kitchen tiles, her body in seemingly neverending raptures of pure pleasure.

When she was done, Bastion clicked his tongue, tutting.

"Pull up your diaper, naughty girl," said Bastion. "Then sit down on that cushion." He pointed at a cushion on a kitchen stool. "And wait for Daddy to bring you dinner."

"But it's not dinner time yet," said Kiera, pulling up her diaper, noticing that her Daddy hadn't told her to remove the dildo yet. Surely she wasn't going to eat dinner while wearing it?

She sat on the stool in her diaper and a Barbie tank top. She had spent the day experimenting with new bubble bath scents, so she was hot and sweaty and had stripped down to the basics. She wore a diaper all the time at home now, since the baby was already putting pressure on her bladder and making her pee a little every time she coughed or sneezed. It had been Bastion's idea, of course, but she had happily agreed to it.

Bastion placed some items on the kitchen counter: a sippy cup, a plastic spoon, and a jar of pureed spinach.

"Ew, spinach," said Kiera.

"It's high in folic acid," said Bastion. "It's good for the baby."

Kiera shuddered, still dealing with the aftershock of her incredible climax, unable to forget it given the large object wedged inside her body.

"Eat up," said Bastion, spoonfeeding her the green mixture.

"Not hungry," said Kiera moodily, pulling away.

"This is the last chance you'll get to eat before bed," Bastion told her. "It's an early bedtime for you today, young lady."

Kiera scowled. "But it's only seven o'clock!"

Bastion pushed more green mixture into her mouth, then he opened another jar and shoved in some mashed-up lentils too.

"Lentils! Yuk!"

"They're good for you, babygirl," he said. "And you'd better eat them all up or your punishment will be even greater."

Kiera stopped resisting and did as she was told, eating all of her food and secretly enjoying the fact that her Daddy was looking after all the baby's nutritional needs.

"Now take a nice big drink of milk," said Bastion, pushing the sippy cup toward her.

Kiera gulped down her milk.

"Good girl," said Bastion. "Now it's bedtime."

"But I'll never sleep like this," said Kiera, pointing down at her diaper. "I'm still wearing the... thing."

"Looks like you're going to have to find a way," said Bastion, groaning slightly as he lifted her off her stool, and cradling her as he carried her upstairs. "You obviously enjoy wearing the plug, so you're going to have to keep wearing it until Daddy says you can take it out."

Kiera pouted. "Not fair."

"Oh dear, you're starting to get heavy for Daddy," Bastion panted at the top of the stairs.

He placed her down in her cot in her new nursery, which was much bigger and more colorful than the old one. Then, he put her stuffie, Blinky, next to her.

"Daddy," she whispered. "I'll never sleep in a million years. I feel like I want to come again. I'll just be touching myself all night."

"No you won't," said Bastion, taking a pair of handcuffs out of his pocket and threading them through the bars of the cot. Quick as a flash, he yanked her wrists over her head, attaching her arms to the cot rails.

"I... need to... pee..." said Kiera.

"You're wearing a diaper," said Bastion softly.

Kiera huffed and puffed, but she couldn't hold in her pee for long. Somehow, she managed to do it with the thick dildo inside her pussy, and she felt the warmth spread around her diaper.

"I really think I'm too turned on for this," Kiera said, wriggling.

"Oh dear," said Bastion, unsympathetically, but with a mischievous grin. "How will you cope?"

He dragged a futon beside the cot and lay down on it, then started to read a bedtime story about a prince who loved a princess so deeply that he walked through a haunted forest to rescue her, defeating all the scary beasts along the way.

Kiera found it very romantic, and she couldn't help wriggling her butt around, squirming in her diaper as he read it to her. But eventually, she noticed how sleepy she was, and she started to yawn. There was something nice, when she was this tired, about her pussy and asshole being completely filled up. And when Bastion put a thick, bulbous pacifier in her mouth, she found herself drifting off to sleep, full and happy.

*

An early bedtime means an early wake time, but when Kiera opened her eyes at five o'clock, Bastion was already up beside her.

"God, you look beautiful," he said. "You were writhing around making these lovely contented noises all night. Did it feel good, darling? Did you have a good sleep?"

Kiera still had the pacifier in her mouth, but Bastion pulled it out for her and she smiled.

"Yes Daddy," she said. "It felt very good. But... I'm still very, very horny." Bastion kneeled on the bed beside her, and she noticed that he wasn't wearing any boxers. His cock was solid as steel.

"Suck this for five minutes," he said, "and then Daddy will help you with your problem."

Kiera opened her mouth, which had already been stretched so wide by the pacifier, and she let her Daddy slide his long hot dog down the back of her throat.

Bastion fucked her in the mouth, slow and deep, moaning as he did so. She longed to touch him, but her arms were still handcuffed to the cot rails.

"Good girl," he said when he decided that she had sucked him for long enough. He pulled his cock out of her mouth and then yanked down her diaper, which was heavy with wetness, but he didn't seem to mind.

He angled the plug so that it slipped out of her asshole, but he twisted it round so that her pussy was still full.

Then, he lifted her butt in the air and pressed his cock against her asshole.

"Been thinking about this all night," he said, as he squeezed his dick into her ass. "Hot fucking damn."

"Oh god," Kiera panted, her heavy breasts jiggling up and down as Bastion fucked her in the ass. The dildo wiggled about in her pussy and Bastion took hold of it, starting to slide it in and out of her, in time with his dick.

"I'm gonna put so much cum in your ass you're gonna have to wear another diaper to stop it squirting out all over the floor," Bastion panted.

"That's okay," panted Kiera. "I'll wear anything you want me to wear, Daddy. And that's a promise."

On hearing her words, Bastion grabbed hold of her butt, thrusting his dick deep inside her and coming with all his might. Then, keeping her pinned in that position, he fucked her with the dildo, sliding it against her clit until she came so hard she screamed.

After, Bastion unlocked the handcuffs and held her in his arms.

"Daddy's taking the day off work today," he said. "There's something important I need to show you."

"Something else?" Kiera said. Bastion was so full of surprises. He grabbed her a clean diaper and then took her over to the window. "See that building over there?" he said, pointing.

"The hotel?" It wasn't the hotel that had paid for the exclusive use of her bubble baths, which had already started putting ludicrous sums of money into her bank account. This was a different hotel, but still a fancy one.

"Yes," said Bastion. "I bought it yesterday."

"You did?"

"Yeah," said Bastion. " I'm turning it into a homeless shelter. Thought we might call it 'Kiera's Place'."

Kiera immediately turned to Bastion with tears in her eyes. "Oh Daddy," she said. "That's the best gift you've ever given me."

Chapter Twenty-Two

BASTION

K IERA MADE THE MOST beautiful bride in the world. She wore a long cream dress with wildflowers sewn into it. And as she had said her vows to Bastion, his heart had almost exploded with happiness.

They had gotten married in an enchanted forest. Not a real one of course, but decorated to look like one, with fairy lights strung between the lush green trees, and centerpieces of ivy and branches, with flickering orbs and sparkling decorations.

Even the food was forest-inspired, with wild mushroom risotto and mocktails made of foraged herbs. A musician played enchanting melodies on a harp nearby, and everything felt truly perfect.

Bastion stood at Kiera's side, cupping her hands in his. "I hope you're enjoying today as much as I am," he said to her.

"It's the best day of my life," Kiera said back to him. "Thank you, Daddy. For all of it. For being you. For making us *us*."

Bastion smiled. He was about to say something soppy and romantic, but just then, Daisy and Peach, who were dressed as woodland nymphs, ran up to them.

"The raspberry mocktail is so yummy!" said Daisy, giggling. "I know it's alcohol-free, but I feel... giddy!"

Kiera laughed, her beautiful cheek dimples on display. It was so good to see her getting on so well with her friends. They were both already married, and they'd had their happy-ever-afters, which meant that all three of them could be pleased for one another as equals.

"Didn't have you down as a fairytale type person," Daisy said to Kiera, poking her round, eight-months-pregnant tummy.

"Nor did I," she said with a giggle.

"Sometimes I worry that it all seems too good to be true," Daisy said with a sigh, her voice a little softer now. "I get scared that the fairytale will end and Montague will wake up one day and leave me."

Kiera reached out and grasped Daisy's hands in hers. "You just have to believe," she said. "The world is a good place. Good people are out there. We all deserve goodness."

Daisy smiled, her eyes shining. "Montague is good," she said. "And so is Bastion."

Bastion, who had been pretending not to listen, looked up at the mention of his name. He gave Daisy a reassuring smile. "We're all happy here," he said, his voice soft and comforting. "And we'll stay that way."

Daisy and Peach had tears in their eyes and Kiera took them both in her arms.

"We'll get through anything together," she said. "Just like we always have."

The friends hugged each other tight and let out a cheer.

"Long live happily ever afters!"

"By the way," said Peach, who had given birth to her triplets now, "have you got a name for the baby yet?"

"We have," said Kiera, smiling up at Bastion. "We're going to call her Hope."

"Tad's chosen a middle name too," said Bastion, looking over at his son proudly. Tad had been his best man today, and was happily chatting with the other guests at the wedding. "He's gone with June, after the month he was born. A cute little way of connecting them."

"That's so lovely," said Peach. "It's perfect."

As the four of them stood there, surrounded by magical trees and the enchanted sunset, Bastion felt like this was better than any fairytale he'd ever read... because it was real.

*

"Sorry we couldn't get married in a bounce house," said Bastion, when they were back in their new home after a long and wonderful day. "Probably not the best idea when you're heavily pregnant."

"It's okay," said Kiera. "This was better. You're my handsome prince, after all."

Bastion smiled. He felt like a prince when he was with Kiera. He felt good and young.

"There *is* one type of bouncing you're allowed to do," he said, his expression suddenly serious.

"There is, Daddy?" asked Kiera.

"Sure," replied Bastion. He lay back on the bed and instructed Kiera to straddle him. "You can bounce on Daddy."

"That's very naughty, Dadddy," said Kiera, reaching into his pants and pulling out his already thick erection.

Then, as she slid down onto him and began to bounce, she smiled. "That feels so good."

Bastion smiled too.

Happy endings did exist. And with every happy ending, there came a new beginning.

ele

Thanks so much for reading! I loved writing the chemistry between Kiera and Bastion in this novel. Two wounded souls, lashing out at the world because they don't want to get hurt. Rather than focusing on making them enemies for too long, I wanted to show how sweet both characters could be around one another. And how steamy things could get — fast! I've never written a one-night stand DDlg novel before. I know strictly speaking Kiera and Bastion didn't have full-blown sex in the castle, but it was still a pretty hot (and cold!) encounter, right?

*If you enjoyed reading this book as much as I enjoyed writing it, please **give me a review**! Every review means so much, and helps other people find new books to love and cherish! :)*

Head over here to read a bonus epilogue featuring Bastion and Kiera! It shows them taking a dirty weekend... in Scotland!

And if you haven't read the rest of the Daddies Inc series yet, check it out!

Plus... keep in touch!

*Don't forget to find me on **Facebook**! And join my **readers' group** for maximum Lucky fun!*

Lucky x o x

P. S. Looking for your next book? **Visit my website** for a full list of my series and take your pick!

Also By Lucky Moon

BAD BOY DADDIES

LIBERTY LITTLES

DADDY SAVES CHRISTMAS (IN A LITTLE COUNTRY CHRISTMAS)

SECOND CHANCE DADDIES

DADDY'S GAME

THE DADDY CONTEST

DADDY'S ORDERS

DRIFTERS MC

DADDY DEMANDS

DADDY COMMANDS

DADDY DEFENDS

DADDIES INC

BOSS DADDY

YES DADDY

MORE DADDY

COLORADO DADDIES

HER WILD COLORADO DADDY

FIERCE DADDIES

THE DADDIES MC SERIES

DANE

ROCK

HAWK

DADDIES MOUNTAIN RESCUE

MISTER PROTECTIVE

MISTER DEMANDING

MISTER RELENTLESS

SUGAR DADDY CLUB SERIES

PLATINUM DADDY

CELEBRITY DADDY

DIAMOND DADDY

CHAMPAGNE DADDY

LITTLE RANCH SERIES

DADDY'S FOREVER GIRL

DADDY'S SWEET GIRL

DADDY'S PERFECT GIRL

DADDY'S DARLING GIRL

DADDY'S REBEL GIRL

MOUNTAIN DADDIES SERIES

TRAPPED WITH DADDY

LOST WITH DADDY

SAVED BY DADDY

STUCK WITH DADDY

TRAINED BY DADDY

GUARDED BY DADDY

STANDALONE NOVELS

PLEASE DADDY

DDLG MATCHMAKER SERIES

DADDY'S LITTLE BRIDE

DADDY'S LITTLE REBEL

DADDY'S LITTLE DREAM

VIGILANTE DADDIES

BLAZE

DRAKE

PHOENIX

Copyright